WHAT MONSTERS DO

D1516459

Nichola

To Thomas
It is not our
flesh . . . .

Nichola Prince

Bibliofear

* * *

Bibliofear
13 Macclesfield Road
LONDON
SE25 4RY

First published in the UK by Bibliofear 2012

ISBN-13: 978-1479108381 (paperback)
ISBN-10: 1479108383 (paperback)

Contents

Acknowledgements

My sincerest thanks go to the following for their help in preparing this volume:

Marie O'Regan for encouragement and editorial support.

Craig Burman-Vince for proof reading and being wonderful.

Carlos Castro for creating a cover which I find genuinely disturbing and beautiful.

For more on Carlos go to **skizoart.blogspot.fr** or email him at **Carlos9@hotmail.fr**

John Bolton for his painting, The Princess and the Satyr which inspired 'The Beast in Beauty'. For more details see 'works > short stories' on www.nicholasvince.com. Check out John's website **www.johnbolton.com** or follow him on twitter on **@boltonstudio**

Ben Vince for advice on the workings of the NHS and everyone at *Retreats for You* for their encouragement; for 'The Worst Day'.

———————

For more information please see
www.nicholasvince.com

Follow on Twitter:
@nicholas_vince

Family Tree

The email's subject read: 'Hi Bryan, it's me, Adrian. I have a favour to ask.'

I dropped the coffee I was holding and stood up, looking down at the mess on my desk, my shirt, tie, trousers.

Kevin, who sits next to me at work, said, 'Oh, mate! What's happened?' He was smiling, concerned.

I pointed at the screen and said: 'Read the subject of the fourth email down, the one highlighted.' He did so and turned to look at me.

'Uh, is Adrian your secret boyfriend?'

'No, doofus. He's my brother.'

'Oh, family, eh? What's he want, money? Come on, let's get you cleaned up. I can't help with your trousers, but I've got a shirt and tie you can borrow.'

I started walking to the kitchen area with him, so we could grab paper towels.

'Kevin,' I said, 'I haven't seen Adrian in nearly twenty-five years.'

'Wow. How come?'

'When my parents separated, he went with Dad—to Australia. A sheep farm. Really isolated. Look, I'll tell you over lunch.'

When I'd changed my shirt and tie, I read the rest of the email, with the damp trousers clinging to my thighs. Adrian said he wanted to buy me dinner so we could

catch up. He wanted to meet as soon as possible and said
he'd be checking his emails throughout the day. I didn't
reply. I dragged the email to the trash folder, right clicked
that and emptied it. I wanted nothing to do with him.
Not after what he'd done.

At lunch, Kevin and I grabbed a quiet table in the pub
and I waited whilst Kevin ordered our meals and drinks
at the bar. I tried to remember the last time I'd thought
of Adrian. Days, months, years? I realised I'd cut my
brother from my mind. My grudge against him was all I
remembered. The regret I felt chilled me.

'Mate, you're crying,' said Kevin, as he sat down.

'What?' I said, looking up. 'Oh, yes. Sorry, sorry.
Didn't mean to. Give me a minute.'

I fumbled for my hanky, remembered I'd used it to
mop up the spilled coffee, wiped my eyes anyway and
blew my nose.

'Take your time, mate, you've obviously had a shock.'

'OK, here it is,' I said. 'Mum and Dad, well it was
messy. Nastily messy and sudden. It was a day or two
after our thirteenth birthday. There was an argument.
Adrian and I, we heard parts of it in our bedroom. I can
remember Dad saying: "Well, it's got to be one of them
and I think it's Adrian." I really didn't understand what
Adrian might have done. You see, we were, I mean *are*,
twins. Pretty inseparable. I kept on asking him what it
was he'd done, but he denied doing anything. I got really
angry with him. I think I started punching him. I mean
he was my twin—we loved each other, and I felt he was
holding out on me. It sounded as if the trouble was his
fault and I couldn't trust him any more.

'Then Mum told Dad, really screamed at him, that he
had to leave and take Adrian with him. She didn't want
anything to do with either of them. I haven't seen them
since. If Dad sent cards for my birthday or Christmas, I

never saw them.'

'Wait a minute,' said Kevin. 'When you say, you *loved* each other … you don't mean …?'

'What? You listened to all that and that's what you got? Will you get your mind out of porn sites?'

'I just wanted to be clear, that's all,' he said, grinning.

'Kevin, I really don't think you're taking my pain seriously.'

'Just trying to get the whole picture, mate,' he said, making a calming gesture with his hands.

I thought about it and then leaned across the table to him. 'OK, does watching your brother jerk off count as wrong?'

He giggled. 'I knew it!' he said, flicking his hand in triumph.

'Sshh! Jesus, why am I telling you this?'

'Mate, it's OK. Really. Go on. What happened then?'

'Next day, Dad and Adrian were gone. Mum wouldn't talk about it. We moved out a couple of weeks later and came down here to London. It was like she was so busy organising the move, she didn't have time to talk about them. I tried asking a few times, but she just told me it was better this way. She didn't say it outright, but I still had the impression it was Adrian's fault he and Dad had to leave. She lost or removed all photos of them during the move. I remember her telling me I was thirteen and old enough to be the man of the house. How old fashioned is that?'

'So, what did the email say? What favour does Adrian want?' said Kevin.

'He didn't say. He's asked to meet me. Up in town.'

'What have you told him?'

'I haven't yet.'

I realised I didn't know if I could get the email back, now I'd deleted it.

'But you're going to?' said Kevin.

'Why do I have the feeling that you're only asking because of a prurient curiosity about my brother?'

'Oh, yeah,' he said, nodding enthusiastically.

When I got back to the office, I'd received another email from Adrian. He said he thought I might have deleted the first one or it hadn't got through and just in case, he'd written again.

I emailed Adrian that I'd meet him the next day. I wanted time to digest this. Really, I guess, I needed time to work out how I felt about him. And to remember. Twenty-five years is a long time. Of course I'd missed him at first, but I'd always believed he was to blame for him and Dad having to leave. Then, I just got on with my life.

I spent most of the afternoon trying to piece memories together. I was saddened at how few incidents I recalled clearly.

When I got home I waited until the kids had gone to bed before explaining what had happened to Evelina, my wife. She asked if I wanted her to go with me. I loved her for asking and I thought about it, but decided against it. Something inside said, that if I decided I didn't want to see Adrian afterwards and they hadn't met, it would be easier.

As I brushed my teeth that evening, for a moment, I thought: 'How will I recognise him?' Then it struck me how stupid I was being. I was looking at his face in my own mirror. We were born identical twins. He couldn't have changed that much.

Adrian had chosen a small bar in the heart of Soho. It was crowded, even on a Tuesday. I guess they all are.

He was sitting at a table by himself, watching the door. In other words, he'd made sure that once I was over the threshold, he'd see me. He had no intention of letting me decide to run.

Life had not been kind to his – our – face. There were long scars at the corners of his mouth, which went up to his ears on either side. I wondered who'd used a knife on him like that. His hair was long and when he stood to greet me, I could see he'd obviously worked out more than I had. Then I realised it was probably from working outdoors on the farm.

'Hello Bryan,' he said, opening up his arms to hug me as I extended my right hand to shake his. We paused, neither quite knowing what to do, but after a moment he smiled and then took my hand in both of his. I noticed that the cuticles of his nails were red raw.

'Thank you for coming. It means a lot, really does,' he said. 'Here, let me get you a drink.'

I could have run then, I suppose. I still wasn't sure I'd actually go for dinner with him. Part of me just wanted to hit him, to let out all the previously forgotten rage and blame I felt for him.

'How's Mum?' he asked.

'She's living in Brighton. Is that the favour you want from me? To see if you can get back into her good books?'

'No, it's not that, though I would like to see her again.'

'What, then?'

'Listen Bryan, can't we talk for a bit? I mean we've got a lot of catching up to do——'

'Whose fault is that?'

'Bryan, please, I can explain everything, really. But not here. Please, let's have the meal and I can tell you why it all happened. You want to know, don't you?'

I thought about it for a few seconds. 'Yes, I want to know.'

As we walked, he explained how he'd found where I'd

worked on the internet, via the company website.

He led the way to a nearby Chinese restaurant, where he'd booked a small private room, at the top of a narrow flight of stairs. I wondered if it was more usually used by business men or courting couples.

We ordered the food, and waited for it to be served before we spoke properly again.

'I'm ill, Bryan, that's why we had to leave.'

'What? That doesn't make sense. Mum wouldn't have thrown you both out because of an illness.'

'No, listen. It was Dad's fault. He hadn't told her until that evening. It's a kind of genetic defect which only appears in twins every so often. He knew about it because his grandfather had suffered. He didn't want to tell Mum, even when we were born, as he couldn't be certain one of us would be affected.'

'Back up. We're identical twins, Adrian. We come from the same egg, surely we should both suffer from this disease.'

He put his chopsticks down and looked at me.

'Identical twins don't share exactly the same genetic makeup and … there is magic in this dull world,' he said.

'What?'

He sighed.

'Bryan, I've been over this a hundred times in my head and there isn't an easy way to say this. I don't think you'll believe me, but you have to try. For the sake of your sons, you have to try.'

'What about my sons?'

'Bryan, what do you know about our family name?'

'Lycoan. It comes from the area of Arcadia in Greece. There's some legend about a king who wanted to test whether or not his guest was really a god; Zeus, I think. He did so by killing one of his fifty sons and serving parts of him mixed into a dish of meats. Which is completely illogical. So, what? Are you telling me you're a cannibal. That's your sickness? That's just … uh, sick.'

'No Bryan, I'm not saying that. Think of the punishment which Zeus gave Lycoan.'

The twins had looked up the story on Wikipedia when they'd done family names for a school project. The punishment of Zeus was to turn Lycoan into a wolf. Hence, lycanthropy.

I laughed. 'You can't be serious? You're trying to tell me that you're what, a werewolf?'

'I'm trying to tell you that I am … and one of your twins may be too.'

'You're right, you are ill, and I can see why Mum didn't want anything to do with either you or Dad. You're sick in the head, that's all. Just sick in the head!'

I stood to leave and walked to the door, but he was there before me. With his back to it, he turned a key I hadn't noticed before.

'Stay back, I promise I won't hurt you, but you have to see.'

He bent his head forward slightly and brought his hands towards his face. I stepped back further from him as I looked at his nails. They were splitting as claws pushed up from beneath them. Blood oozed and he whimpered in pain.

Then he opened his mouth and put his fingers into it. He pulled down with his left hand and up with his right. At first I thought he was trying to open his jaws wider, but then saw he was pulling the skin from his face and it was parting along those scars at his mouth. There were tearing and sucking sounds as the skin moved beneath his hands. The face beneath was covered in fur matted with blood, and blood filled his eyes. His jaws thrust forward a little, aping the muzzle of a wolf. Fangs pushed between his human teeth, crowding his mouth. He crouched slightly, like an animal ready to spring.

He panted and growled.

'Bryan.' The voice was guttural and indistinct, because of those too many teeth. 'Do you see now?'

'Yes, yes. Please stop.'

He used both hands to reach behind his head to pull his face back into place, like a man pulling on a wetsuit hood.

For a few minutes the only sound in the room was us breathing heavily, and squelching noises as he pushed the flesh back into place. The scars at his mouth were now red raw.

'You don't need a full moon then?' I said.

'At the full moon, I have no choice. Then I have to eat as the wolf.'

'Does it have to be human?'

'No, but at full moon I have less control over what or who I'll attack. That's why Dad took me to the outback, to a sheep station.'

He talked about his life, how each twenty-nine and a half days he would go into a cage with a fully grown sheep. How over the years, the cage had been expanded, the walls made taller and eventually a roof added to ensure he didn't get out amongst the entire flock. The number of sheep had grown over time from one to half a dozen.

He was kept from the world for most of his life; his schooling had come over radio and television. Dad was his only friend and jailer. Eventually, in his early twenties, he'd been allowed to visit town and meet girls, but he realised he couldn't face falling in love and trying to explain what happened to him. He contented himself with molls, as he called them.

It occurred to me, I hadn't asked about Dad and how he was. Adrian told me he'd died, killed a week ago in a bar fight.

'The bastard died before he could keep his promise to me,' said Adrian.

'What promise is that?'

'To kill me. That's the favour I want from you, Bryan. I want you to kill me, with this.'

He reached up to his throat and undid the choker he was wearing. It was a thin chain with a silver bullet hanging from it.

'You want me to kill you with jewellery?' I said.

'It's possible to do it by cutting my head off, but I think you might muck that up. It's not easy, you know, cutting off someone's head. You need to have strong arms and a sharp blade. With Mary Queen of Scots, it took them three blows.'

'Why me?'

'It's part of the curse laid by Zeus. I can only die if it's done by someone who loves me. Suicide isn't allowed. I've tried. He was a right bastard, that Zeus.'

'This is madness,' I said. 'They didn't have silver bullets in ancient Greece.'

'No, it would have been a sword or dagger, but I didn't think you'd want to get that close and personal. Don't worry, I'm not expecting you do it here and now. There's too many witnesses, you'd never get away with it. I thought we could drive out to Dartmoor or the Scottish Highlands. It'll mean being away from home for a couple of nights, but I'm sure Evelina will understand.'

He paused.

'If it's any help, I have to be the wolf, not me when it's done.'

I don't know what revolted me most, the thing he was asking me to do or the calm way he was explaining it to me. I felt sick, and had to get out of the room. Pushing him to one side, I wrenched the locked door open and ran down the stairs, leaving him to explain to the waiters what had happened to their door.

Outside it was dark and raining and the cold water helped clear my head. I ran to Hyde Park and then walked for an hour or so in the pouring rain. I half-expected Adrian to appear; I wondered if his illness gave him special tracking skills.

Soaked to the skin, I headed home, wondering why I hadn't asked him the most obvious question.

The next morning, I turned on the computer as soon as I got out of bed, eager to check the time of the next full moon. It was in two days, at the weekend. I also started researching the genetics of twins and hereditary diseases.

Evelina came into the room and put her arms around my shoulders.

'How did it go last night, with Adrian? Only, you're going to be late for work,' she said.

'All he's interested in, is getting some money from me. He's a drunk, really, so I won't be seeing him again.'

After breakfast, as I left the house, I kissed my ten year old daughter Marianne on the top of her head goodbye. Rupert and Trevor well, they're twelve now, so no kiss. I hesitated, looking at them, then tousled their hair, as I usually did. But, Evelina was busy with school bags so I just shouted 'bye' and left. I didn't kiss her goodbye. When did we stop doing that?

When I arrived at work, Kevin and I were the only ones in. He placed a cup of coffee on my desk and sat on the edge, grinning at me.

'Before you ask, I don't think I can talk about it. Not yet. Sorry, mate.'

'No problem,' he said. I smiled my appreciation as he looked concerned, rather than disappointed.

We hardly spoke all day and I worked through lunch

so I could leave early.

When I got through the front door at home, I could hear voices in the lounge and then Evelina laughed. I hung my coat and walked in.

Adrian sat on the sofa, with a cup of tea in his hand. Marianne got up from the floor and rushed to me; to give my usual hug. She excitedly showed me the book on Australian animals she'd received as a gift from Adrian. I saw the twins were both holding boomerangs and wore stockman's hats.

Evelina rose from the sofa and showed me her opal bracelet and necklace.

'Hi darling, Adrian dropped by with these wonderful gifts.

'Hello Adrian,' I said. Adrian wouldn't look me in the eye, but raised a hand in greeting.

'Can you give me a hand with dinner, Bryan?' said Evelina.

I followed her into the kitchen.

When I'd closed the kitchen door, Evelina said: 'He's not really a drunk, is he?'

'How long's he been here?'

'About half an hour. I invited him for dinner, I mean he is your brother and I don't see how we could simply throw him out. The gifts must have cost a fortune.'

She was very calm and determined that we didn't have a choice but to entertain him. It slowly dawned on me: the gifts for the kids were a little too well chosen, which meant that Evelina had known about Adrian all along. She admitted he'd made contact with her through Facebook and discussed how best to approach me. She'd given him my work email address, so she wouldn't have to be there when I first read his email: scared she'd show no surprise. I assumed she didn't know the real reason he was here.

During the meal Adrian told stories of life in Australia on the sheep station, but also stories of when we were boys. He asked the twins whether or not they ever pretended to be the other, just to confuse people. They cheerfully admitted they did and only regretted that their parents and sister could tell them apart.

Towards the end of the evening, Evelina asked Adrian if he was available to join us over the weekend. We could find an outing for us all. Adrian explained we'd already discussed the possibility of just he and I going away for the weekend and that afterwards, he had to take a ship to Russia. It was a place he'd always wanted to visit. He meant it was a place where he might easily be believed to have disappeared.

Evelina beamed when I said I'd definitely decided Adrian and I should go. I would arrange a day off work on Friday so we could travel up. Adrian suggested we take the overnight train to Inverness on Thursday evening.

My boss was less than sympathetic to the short notice request. I pointed out I worked too many hours anyway and the company owed me at least this much. Kevin volunteered to cover the two meetings I had planned, which probably stopped me from losing my temper and resigning on the spot. I hugged Kevin and whispered thanks in his ear.

'I'll see you on Monday?' he said. He didn't sound certain and neither was I.

It was a bloody awful journey. We had a compartment on the overnight train to ourselves, but I hardly slept.

In Inverness we hired a 4x4 and drove to the holiday cottage Adrian had found us. It was really isolated, with forests all round it and a garden that led down to a loch with black, peat-filled water. There was a boat at the jetty as part of the deal.

We didn't have much to say to each other, but as the afternoon wore on, I asked him, 'Will it be tonight or tomorrow you change? I'm not quite clear what qualifies as a full moon.'

'It'll be tomorrow.'

Then I asked the question I should have asked at the restaurant. 'What if I don't love you enough?'

'What do you mean?' he said.

'I mean, is there some sort of scale my love is measured against? Do I have to complete a questionnaire? Is brotherly love enough? What if I shoot you and it doesn't work? What if I wound you and you're changed? You said yourself, you can't control who you attack. What if it's me who gets killed? What will you do then? Ask Mum? I'll tell you now, she's too frail for this.'

'It's OK, Bryan … I'm scared too, and I really don't know all the answers. Perhaps if you just try to remember when we were boys, before I left. Remember what happened the day you got beaten up by those guys at school. How Mum had to patch you up and put you to bed. Then how you woke in the night, calling for me. How I joined you in bed and held you, whilst you cried and got snot on my pyjamas. You don't have to declare you love me, all you have to do is squeeze the trigger. I think the act itself is proof enough. It's no more effort than pulling the ring on a can.'

On the Saturday Adrian said he needed to buy some things and it was best I stay at the cottage. He wanted me to practise with the gun. I fired half a dozen ordinary shells at a target carved on a log. I never asked him how he'd got the gun, which had a silencer.

He came back in the afternoon with chains. Then he went into the woods and started preparing a clearing. He wound the chains around the trees and made sure they were secure.

When I joined him, just before sunset, with a meal I'd cooked for us, he said: 'One more thing. You'll need to skin me.'

'What?'

'I want you do this as soon as my head and torso are free of my skin. I don't want you to wait for the full transformation.'

'You mean there's more to it than what you showed me at the restaurant?'

'Yes, at full moon, I step out of my entire skin. Dad was always scared I might destroy the skin and never change back, so he always guarded it. But I want you to shoot me once my head and torso are clear. That should be enough. It's important, Bryan, as I'm not sure these chains will hold me if I fully transform. You must kill me once my torso is clear.'

As soon as it started getting dark, he stripped naked and showed me how to operate the handcuffs he'd attached to the chains. Then he sat on a log and we waited.

'Aren't you cold?' I said.

'It won't be for long.'

He looked at his pile of clothes.

'I got you something. It's in my jacket pocket. It's for afterwards, for you and the boys.'

Then he started to change. He stood immediately, looking over the trees at the moon rising above them. He was writhing and gnawed at the chains.

There was enough slack in them for him to repeat the tearing of his human face, but this time there was more urgency. He pulled at his flesh, like you might at clothes which are crushing you.

When the skin was clear of his torso he was growling and snarling at me. He didn't try to speak.

I pointed the gun at him and squeezed the trigger. There was a dull click.

My first thought was he'd tricked me. That this was all a ruse; to get me away from my family so he could feed on me in peace.

I looked at the gun, lit only by the moonlight, trying to work out what was wrong. Then I heard the first of the chains snap as he lunged towards me. His mouth with its mixture of canine and human teeth gaped and gnashed at me.

I felt the gun, checking the safety catch was off and realised the magazine wasn't pushed all the way home. The other chain on his arm snapped and he lunged at me again, slashing at my face, catching my cheek with claws.

Shocked by the pain, I pointed the gun at him and pulled the trigger. He staggered under the force of the bullet.

'I love you,' I said, as I pulled the trigger again and again, even though I knew there'd been only one bullet.

He lay still, whimpering as he had when he'd changed back at the restaurant. I didn't go near him until he'd been still and quiet for an hour. Then I did as he'd instructed: burned his skin and dumped his wolf body, weighted with stones, in the middle of the loch.

Who knew I had so many tears in me, for someone I hardly knew?

Back in the cottage, I opened the small package he'd left for me. I looked at the thing, though I knew by touch alone.

There is a moment, a single, only just measurable moment; when as you stand the world shifts under your feet. All that was solid liquifies and you find yourself falling into acts which you dread. There is in your life until then and after. Nothing, no minutiae of your life, will match with the person who you knew yourself to be. That person is gone and you're left with only this choking taste of ashes.

The package contained a silver bullet and he'd engraved the name of one of my sons upon it.

Tunes from the Music Hall

It was a dark, damp and foggy afternoon in London. At five o'clock the lamplighter passed around Thornton Square lighting the street lamps, leaving globes of yellow brilliance in his wake. The fine mist of the fog settled on his coat and hat; glistening in the lamplight, so he shimmered gold. As he walked, he whistled tunes he'd heard in the music hall. I waited for him each day, singing the words to those I knew and making up lyrics for those new to me.

A brougham, pulled by a black mare, drew up outside the house. I assumed they had the wrong address, as the house received so very few visitors. The coachman hurried to open the door to allow the passengers to alight. The first was someone I knew, Mr Albright, the estate agent. He's a man in his fifties, and he wheezed as he stepped onto the pavement. He was followed by a young man in his twenties. He carried himself proudly and waited for Mr Albright to open the front door. He studied the façade of the house and then surveyed the square before entering.

Albright opened the door and walked to the hall stand, where there was an oil lamp. It took him a few moments to light it. As the young man walked into the house I came down the stairs to get a closer look at him. The oil lamp illuminated the entrance hall and I could see he was a handsome chap.

'As I said sir,' said Albright. 'There is no gas supply at the present, but that can be arranged should you decide to take the property.'

Albright lifted the lamp and began the tour of the empty rooms. I followed them, laughing out loud at some of Albright's descriptions. I think the young man was sometimes amused too, as I caught him smiling to himself behind Albright's back. They were about twenty minutes in the house and at the front door I heard the young man saying that he would take the property. I danced through every room in the house in celebration.

Two servants and furniture arrived a week before the family. There was Rose, the house maid. She was a young, sparky thing. The cook Edith, was a jovial woman and a great admirer of Marie Lloyd. One evening, in the kitchen, I watched entranced as she sang "The Boy I Love", recreating Marie's gestures very well.

The family arrived on the Friday and there was an unfortunate incident. I was very eager to see them, to know who they were, so I stood on the landing overlooking the hall and the front door. The young man, Rudolph, entered with his wife, Bella, and their daughter, Victoria. She was a little poppet aged four, wearing a blue velvet dress. She was very excited to enter her new home and ran away from the door, into the drawing room, squealing with delight. Within a minute she rushed from that room to the dining room on the other side of the hall.

'Mamma,' she called. 'It's wonderful, there are so many pretty things.'

Her mother was still removing her hat and cloak and handing them to Rose. Victoria ran back into the hall and then up the stairs. That is when she saw me and screamed. My face is terrible and I could not blame her.

'What is it Victoria?' said her mother.

The child ran to bury her face in her mother's dress, and pointed back at me.

'That man has a horrible face.'

I was standing by a statue, placed at the corner of the landing on the stairs. It was of an elven creature, fashioned as a stand to hold an oil lamp.

'It must be that statue,' said her father. 'No matter. I'll have it moved into my study. Bella, you must be more sensitive, when choosing these things.'

'Yes, Rudolph.'

I fled to the attic, determined not to approach the child or its nursery. I was greatly saddened by this, as I'd often watch the children play in the gardens which lie at the centre of the square. I loved the songs they sang and I'd hoped to watch Victoria play in the nursery.

It was a quiet household. Rudolph was a writer of mystery novels, which meant he shut himself in his study and demanded the house be almost silent whilst he was working. Therefore, Bella often took Victoria out of the house to theatres and museums. I felt sorry for her, as being unable to receive very many visitors, she was deprived of normal society.

Two months after their arrival they left for a holiday in Italy. The house was quiet for three weeks. I felt these weeks of solitude more deeply than any since I died here.

When they returned, Victoria was her usual cheerful, noisy self. However, Bella seemed despondent. A distance had grown between her and Rudolph. He was distracted. In his study he would place his pen on the desk and stare out the window for long periods.

Two weeks later, on the Thursday, the servants left the house for their weekly afternoon off. Rudolph was in his study on the first floor and in a bad temper. He was late in delivering a short story to a magazine. Bella was chiding Victoria, who was refusing to leave her nursery, as she didn't want to go into the damp streets. I listened outside the nursery door to Bella's entreaties and promises. These proved ineffectual attempts to persuade Victoria to leave. I heard her finally threaten to fetch Rudolph. Victoria quietened.

There was a determined knocking at the front door. After giving Victoria stern warnings to stay quiet, Bella reluctantly left the nursery to open the door. A young man, Italian by name, Angelo Saverilli, came into the house without a formal invitation and stood in the hallway, removing his gloves and placing his hat and cane on the hall table. He had long black hair and dark seductive eyes.

'Bella, what a charming home you have made here. It is bellissima.'

'Conte Saverilli. This is an unexpected visit.'

I noticed she didn't invite him into the drawing room.

'How long have you been in England?' she said.

'Hours, mere hours. Nothing could keep me from visiting my new friends Bella and Rudy. Where is he? In the study upstairs?'

'Yes, but he's writing and doesn't like to be disturbed Conte—'

'Nonsense! For a new friend like me, I'm sure he'll be delighted.'

He bounded past her and ran up the stairs to find Rudolph standing at the door of his study. Rudolph looked at Angelo and I couldn't tell if he was pleased to see him or not. Angelo walked up to him and placed his hands on his shoulders. He gently pushed Rudolph back into the study, releasing him so that he could close the study door behind them. Then he walked to the chaise longue and sat upon it.

Rudolph stared angrily at Angelo. He moved to stand in front of him.

'How dare you Angelo? I thought we agreed … I thought never to see you again.'

'I know Rudy, I know. Bella poisoned you against me. Against us.'

'Angelo, you do not understand, our friendship … here, it is illegal. They passed a law, we could go to prison.'

'How can love be illegal?'

Angelo took Rudolph's right hand in his and kissed the palm. Rudolph groaned and I saw tears in his eyes. His shoulders drooped and he sank to his knees. He took Angelo's face in his hands and they kissed passionately. Angelo reached for Rudolph's shirt buttons, but Rudolph held his hands.

'No. Not now,' Rudolph said.

'Then there will be a time?'

'Yes. Go now and I will telegraph you at your hotel.'

Angelo smiled and took his leave. As he passed Bella in the hall, I think he felt sorry for her, as he bowed his head and smiled sadly at her; the pitying smile of the triumphant.

She looked up to see Rudolph standing on the landing. As she approached him, he walked to his study and locked the door behind him. I joined him there as he paced, re-read his story, tore it repeatedly, wept and eventually sat on the chaise longue, his head in his hands.

I knew that passion; that terrible, overwhelming desire for a single person that accepts no dispute. How could I not? That is why I died here.

I was nineteen and beautiful. I played juvenile leads in the West End of London. Cole was thirty with tender blue eyes, broad shoulders and a fine waist. He was the most popular leading man of the day.

When we first met at rehearsals, he shook my hand

and smiled at me. He held my hand for longer than I expected, searching my eyes. I could smell his cologne and I found it intoxicating. I blushed, at which he smiled more broadly and then winked. During the rehearsal period, I visited him at his home.

Once the performances started, we often dined after the show, at the *Savoy*. One night, after we'd drunk substantially, he invited me to a house in Cleveland Street. I'd heard of the place and knew there were many telegraph boys and men from The Horse Guards there; available for hire. On our entering for the first time, Cole was immediately hailed by a striking youth, with oiled brown hair. Cole introduced me to Perry and asked him if he would spend the night with us, in a private room.

Perry said, 'You never asked me to share you before. He must be something special to you.'

Cole smiled and said, 'He is.'

I was confused. I did not want to share Cole either, but if it meant being with him, then I was prepared to accept this.

Thus we continued for some weeks. Around the theatre, we were discreet, but as I moved around back stage, I would know where Cole had walked, as the smell of his cologne lingered. Encountering it; at once my passion and desire for him would be inflamed. I was lost to him and I knew in his way, he loved me.

At Cleveland Street, it became obvious that Cole had become bored with Perry and although he kept me with him always, we tried a succession of young men. Each time we entered the establishment, I was more acutely aware of the whispered jealousies we were creating. Perry and other lads we had dallied with huddled in a corner of the parlour and I saw their dark looks of hatred. Cole was oblivious.

One Sunday, I spent the day alone in this house. I kept

only a cook and she was away that night as her sister was with child and needed her. I dined alone, returning around nine o'clock.

There had been an ugly scene at Cleveland Street the previous night and I had resolved to tell Cole I was no longer willing to visit the place.

At nine-thirty I was startled by the bell at the front door. At once my heart leapt as I imagined only Cole would call at this hour. I was mistaken. Perry and two of his cronies, dressed in female attire, bustled in pushing me into the house.

Their intent was soon clear as I was quickly tumbled to the floor. I thought they might simply beat me and, at worst, scar my face.

Perry murdered me.

The afternoon of Angelo's visit, before the servants' return, I listened to the recriminations and blame, the pleas for understanding and promises of discretion. Rudolph said he wanted to keep his family around him, as he loved both Bella and his daughter. Bella said she had little choice. She dare not denounce her husband, as the scandal would not lead to another marriage. She might receive some sympathy, but eventually would be dropped from what little London society she knew.

I cannot say that the home was happy for the next month, but there were no further scenes. Rudolph left the house more frequently, but Angelo did not visit again.

One Thursday afternoon, when Bella had taken Victoria to the zoo, Angelo arrived. Rudolph was disturbed by his attendance upon him. Angelo was charming. He sat where the sun would play on his eyes and hair. He asked Rudolph for money; as his parents were being tiresome and threatening to cut his allowance unless he returned to Italy to marry a rather ugly heiress.

Rudolph was embarrassed. He had to explain the money in the family was Bella's. He had a small income from his writing, but not much. Of course he would give him what he could. Angelo pouted and chided Rudy for not being a man in his own house. Did not the law say that all his wife's income belonged to him, as her husband? Rudolph agreed that it did, but he had promised Bella he would only use his own income on Angelo. That was their agreement for the current arrangements.

'Arrangements can be changed,' said Angelo. As he did so, he removed his jacket and loosened his cravat.

'You mustn't, Angelo', said Rudolph. 'Not here. The servants might hear.'

'It's Thursday afternoon: the servants have their afternoon off. Bella and Victoria will be at the zoo and then they will have tea. Victoria will ask for sticky iced cakes. When she has eaten them, she will lick her fingers clean. Tell me Rudy, do you like sticky cakes?'

He took Rudy's hand and sucked the index finger and then the middle finger.

An hour later he left with the money he'd requested.

The visits on Thursday afternoon became a regular occurrence. Over time, they talked later into the afternoon, discussing how they might be together more often and travelling to Italy. Always, Angelo left with money.

Towards the end of April, Victoria must have said she felt unwell and didn't want cakes, as Bella and she returned earlier than was usual. From the other side of the square, Bella saw Angelo leave.

When she entered the house, Bella called for the servants, to check they had not also returned. She sent

Victoria to her room, telling her to find a nice book to read.

Rudolph was in his study. She entered without knocking, which was unusual, and closed the door behind her. He swung round in his chair, to face her. A gentleman would have risen to greet a lady, but he no longer treated her as such.

'You promised, Rudolph. You promised he would never be here again.'

Confronted by his lie, he remained silent. His silence angered her even more.

'Damn you Rudolph, damn you and your kind. You sodomite! You're less than a man; you cannot even earn enough to support your family. We live on my money and precious little of it is spent on this family.'

She sobbed for a moment, and then gathered more strength, cutting him as he spoke.

'I'm tired, Rudolph, tired. Tired of this charade which you've forced me into. I've never spoken of Angelo to anyone. I've acted the dutiful wife, raised our daughter, spoken my praise of your writing. Your writing. Hah! It earns us a pittance. Tell me, Rudolph, how many stories have you sold? Does anyone care for your work?'

At that moment, I saw it in his face. The guilt and pity he felt for her, for the life he'd given her was replaced by dark anger. She had mortally wounded him, snubbed his dreams. His face hardened with shame and I saw hatred flower there.

'Listen to me, Rudolph. No more, do you hear me? I'll have no more of this life. You will be a proper husband. You will do your duty by me, as you did for me to have Victoria. There will be no more Angelo. You will never see him again. You will find a job, Father will help you; we will have more children. We will enjoy soirées and dinner parties and there will be people in this house. We will no longer live under the tyranny of your pen and there will be no Angelo!'

He rose from the chair and she shrank back from him, expecting a blow. He reached down to his desk and lifted a silver cigarette case. He stared at her whilst he lit a cigarette.

'Who is Angelo?' he said.

She frowned.

'Your friend, your lover,' she said, almost choking over the last word.'

'I know no-one by that name.'

Hope lit her face as she imagined she had won.

'My dear Bella. This is so sad, you're imagining people. Tell me, can you remember discussing this Angelo with anyone?'

'No. We agreed, that day he came here.'

'No-one visited us, Bella. You know I don't allow visitors, I need quiet for my work.'

'What do you mean?' she said.

'Well, I'm afraid I've seen it in our daughter, too. Do you know she still insists there is a man with a horrible face, who no-one can see, but her? I fear the insanity you suffer from, has been passed to our daughter.'

'No! He lies!' I cried, desperate to help her.

Bella suddenly looked at me. Rudolph followed her gaze.

'He's lying, there is an Angelo!' I said, stepping forward. I knew I could save her, knew I could convince her that she hadn't imagined Angelo.

Bella screamed, backing away from me. I did not understand why. I wanted to save her, so I stepped forward. She groaned, a low despairing sound. I realised then, I had forgotten my face.

When Perry and his friends killed me, they held me down. They pinched my nose, so that I had to gasp for air. When I did so, they poured hydrochloric acid into my mouth and right eye. He told me he'd left one eye so I could see his beauty and watch him smile as I died. As I spoke again, trying to convince Bella, I heard my voice. The acid burned my tongue and my words were indistinct; I spoke an animal guttural noise.

The servants returned a few moments later. Rudolph called down the stairs for Rose to fetch the doctor and for Edith to help him with his wife. Still I insisted on helping Bella, but the more I tried to tell her she wasn't insane, the more she screamed and the more I sealed her fate.

Eventually, a second doctor was called. They certified Bella insane. Victoria ran from her room when she heard her mother being taken. She stood looking down through the banisters, into the hallway, sobbing and terrified. I hid in the attic, so that Victoria wouldn't suffer her mother's fate.

Bella's sister arrived at eight o'clock and after a brief discussion with Rudolph, she took Victoria with her. The servants went to bed early and Rudolph entered his study, where he opened a bottle of whiskey. He drank greedily from the bottle, then wiping his lips with the back of his hand, he sobbed like a small boy.

'What have I done?' he said out loud.

'Killed the thing you loved,' I said. He must have heard me as he looked round.

'Who's there?'

I understood at last. Guilt and shame must have heightened his senses, as did the joy when Victoria first arrived; as did Bella's anger. He saw me and ran to the study door. I laughed and he heard me. Terror struck, he pulled open the door and ran to the landing of the stairs. He looked back to see me standing above him. In a fine dramatic gesture, I had one arm raised and pointed an accusatory finger. I advanced slowly down the stairs towards him, laughing as I did so.

He stepped backwards to escape me and missed the top step. He fell and then tumbled down the stairs to the black and white tiles of the hall, where he smashed his face. I stood over him as he died, accusing him still.

He's here now, in the room which used to be his study. He avoids me, as he says he cannot abide my face. My face is horrific, but they did not harm my body. I still have a beautiful body and one day, when he realises there will only ever be the two of us, he will love me.

I know he will love me.

Green Eyes

Justinian sat watching snow fall. The want of childhood: to dash out and hurl wet, cold missiles at things and people, had long since left him. Even so, he couldn't find it in himself to complain about the snow. He seldom drove the car and when he did, such conditions were a challenge—not a curse. He could still appreciate the sharp, crisp beauty of the whiteness, as long as he was by his log fire; a log fire which was flickering to an end.

Soon, he knew, he'd have to fill the log basket. He shifted on the sofa, wanting to prolong his comfort. He looked down at the cat, a ginger tom, stretched in front of the fire and envied an existence so at peace with assumed comfort.

Dilemma: stay put in the warm, prolonging this as long as possible and perhaps fall asleep and wake to a cold house; or get the logs, stoke the fire, soon be warm again, but also thoroughly disturbed.

He blew a raspberry. These stupid mental games were stealing so much of his time these days. Not senility. Not at fifty-two. Surely?

He laughed, out loud, at himself. The logs had to be got. It was certain. He stood up. Stopped. What was the joke about certainties? Only two certainties in life: death and taxes. But surely, there was a third? Birth: the third certainty.

'He,' would be here soon. Not really a prodigal, but a

son never-the-less.

The cat yawned, stretched, rolled on its back, and presented its tummy for affection. It squirmed on the hearth rug as Justinian regarded it without moving.

He bent and grabbed the cat, threw it on the fire. The smell of burning fur filled the room—each strand with its glowing, coal-red end. Its eyes shrivelled and melted, leaving charred remnants.

Justinian clenched and unclenched his fists as the picture left him. He gently tickled the proffered abdomen.

'I hope you can't read minds, young cat. Besides, I don't think I meant it personally.'

The cat luxuriated in the dying warmth of the fire and the apparent affection of the hand, at which it took the occasional cushioned-pawed swipe.

Logs.

'Must get the logs, oh bright star of the East.' He headed for his jacket and scarf. The cat, still wrapped in the expectation of attention, didn't realise its loss for a few moments. Then, cold green eyes regarded Justinian's receding back. To demonstrate his indifference to this rejection, he licked paw, wiped ear, licked paw, wiped ear and settled to dream of fur, feathers, blood and fear games.

Cold bit sharply at Justinian's cheeks. He walked to the logs, which were a few yards from the back door, listening to the *grunching* of his feet in the snow. A short-handled axe lay embedded in a large stump beside them and he picked it up. He started splitting logs, trying, really trying, not to picture children under the blade. He blinked back tears, not sure if this was emotion or simply the cold.

He looked round him. A couple of inches of snow had fallen already, more on the way. Perhaps He wouldn't make it. Perhaps that would be best. Perhaps if He didn't make it then ... Perhaps. Perhaps. 'Worlds lost in perhaps and if,' he muttered.

He'd forgotten the log basket and he stamped his foot in temper. Concentrate. Damn it. That meant two journeys. He managed to balance five logs, unsafely, in his arms and headed for the door.

Sally was waiting and watching. Slightly amused, slightly exasperated, her dark hair showing, so Justinian claimed, rather attractive flecks of grey. She was sensibly dressed for the weather in tweeds and green boots. Sensible Sally: forty-eight and counting.

'I'll hold the door.' She sounded tense.

He passed her, marvelling at the glow in her green eyes cast from the kitchen light. They still shone, just as they had when—

'Have you got everything I asked for?'

Justinian didn't bother to answer. She knew he had. It was a measure of her nerves that she'd asked. It was explicit in their domesticity that he should do everything she told him. Otherwise, he vaguely realised, she couldn't cope as well as she did.

'The Lockert baby has whooping cough,' Sally said. 'It's that damp house, I expect. Jim Surridge has been promising to fix their guttering since last March—still hasn't bothered. We had a young lad before the bench this morning for stealing a bike, a surly brute, but I think more scared than anything. Judy gave him a proper dressing down when he answered back. The parents actually looked shocked. Alison Farthing fell over outside the Post Office and ...'

So on. Justinian basked in the warm buzz of Sally's voice: half-listening to the lives of people he seldom met and didn't care for. It was part of the ritual as Sally set the kettle on the stove and organised the meal. He put a couple of logs on the fire and the rest in the basket and decided to let fetching more wait. Perhaps He would get them for them.

Justinian could hear Sally well enough in the kitchen from the chair beside the fire.

He rested and watched memories falling behind his eyelids. Her green eyes, glowing in dawn light. Justinian stood beside the bed looking at them.

'Go back to sleep.'

She closed her eyes. He put on jeans and a cheese-cloth shirt. His blond hair reflected in the glass door as he stepped onto the balcony and watched the calm sea.

He turned and looked back at her. She lay under one white sheet and he studied the way it folded around her, breathed with her. The holiday had been fine and now the dawn was so at one with his mind. No birds. No ships. Long empty sands on either side of the beach house. A small wave made a sluggish attempt at breaking the stillness.

Not this morning.

Suddenly Justinian felt a sweet, joyful, desolation that made him want to cry tears of ... what? The whole world was bright and focussed on him and 'real'. For the first time in his life he felt real, part of the world and that at last he was normal.

Confused, he could hardly breathe for the intensity of the emotion. There was a tightness across his chest. He looked through the open door at her and wanted to roll in her arms for comfort, wanted desperately to share the moment. Share it and fix it somehow. He thought he could strangle her, so she wouldn't have to wake to disappointment and regret.

Two gulls crawked and argued over something on the foam. A plane banished the moment utterly. Justinian let her sleep. Perhaps later.

* * *

'Ugh!' said Sally.

The clock struck the half hour. Justinian found himself watching flames.

'What is it?' he called—without moving.

'A rat. It's caught in the trap. It's still alive. Come here, please!'

He moved then. The rat had its forepaw caught. Grabbing the broom, he beat its head.

'OK, stop!'

He was sweating with the exertion.

'You're making a mess. I don't want to be cleaning up blood.'

As he bent down to pick up the rat, the cat got there first and, knowing he'd receive no peace, dragged the carcass and trap out through the cat-flap.

They looked at the smears of red and fur on the floor.

'What time did he say he'd arrive?' said Justinian.

'In about an hour. Clean up the mess and then you can scrape potatoes.'

They didn't speak for some minutes. Justinian looked up from the sink.

'Lo, methinks I hear a horseless carriage.'

'But who would come out on a night ... Oh, it can't be him? Not this early. I haven't got my face on yet. You see who it is. I'm going upstairs to change.'

'Sally, not so sensible,' mumbled Justinian to himself, as he walked through the hall towards the front door.

A tentative knocking, an enquiry, not a summons, met him halfway. Justinian straightened his cravat in the mirror, then opened the door a few inches.

'Yes?' said Justinian.

A young man, mid-twenties, about five foot ten, dark hair sprinkled with snow, camel coat, good looking – very – something about the eyes.

'Excuse me. Is this Firebirch Grange?'

A nicely spoken young man.

'Yes.'

'Ah, good. My name is Davis Land. I've come to see Mrs Sally Kingsmead.'

'Your mother.'

'I think so, yes.'

Shut him out, send him away. Lie, say she died suddenly. Don't let him in.

'Excuse me. Can I come in? Only ...'

'Yes, of course, how very rude.'

Davis made use of the scraper on the porch, to remove the snow on expensive shoes.

'I'm a bit early, I'm afraid.'

'Yes.'

'Thought I'd better leave extra time because of the snow and not knowing where you were. I missed you the first time—ended up in Arundel. Still managed to be early.'

'Let me take your coat.'

'Thanks.'

He wore a suit and silk tie. How sweet, obviously trying to make a good first impression.

'The lounge is through there. There's a fire burning.' Silly fool—what else would a fire do? Justinian hung the coat in the hall and followed Davis into the large lounge. Two sofas faced each other across a coffee table, in the centre of the room.

'Gosh, this is very ... large.'

'Yes, we converted a barn and wanted to give this room a sense of the baronial. Hence this ridiculous fireplace.'

'Er, you haven't introduced yourself.'

'Nor I have. People call me Justinian. It's my name, you know.'

'Er, yes.'

'Then why ask?'

'Sorry?'

'If you knew my name, why did you want to be introduced?'

'Justinian. Stop it,' said Sally, standing in the doorway.

'Forgive him, please. He thinks he's funny, doesn't realise people don't appreciate it. Justinian, have you offered ... Davis, a drink?'

'Remiss of me, I know, but no, I haven't. The lad hasn't even sat down yet, though.'

'Yes, do sit down.'

Davis, finding himself at the end of a sofa, hesitated a moment and then sat. Sally walked past him, to sit opposite, after first evicting the cat.

'What a splendid cat. What's his name?'

'Drink, Mr Land?' Justinian was beside him; obviously trying to be the perfect host. 'I'm sure I can scare up a whiskey or would you prefer tea?'

'Well, whatever everyone is having.'

'Please don't be polite. After all you are, we assume, aux famille. Of sorts.'

'Whiskey, thank you.'

'Justinian get Davis a whiskey, myself a sherry and then get into the kitchen. The meat needs looking at.'

'Perhaps the young man is a vegetarian.'

'No!' Davis was startled by his own voice. 'I'm sorry. I didn't ... No, I'm not a vegetarian.'

'Nor a Buddhist or a Trappist monk,' snapped Sally. 'Justinian, do as you're bid.'

Justinian served the drinks, picked up the cat and sulked into the kitchen, hissing 'Bossy Sally,' under his breath.

'I'm sorry,' said Sally. 'He's just not used to meeting people, new people. He doesn't mean harm.'

Awkward silence, only slightly alleviated by Davis giving what he hoped was an understanding smile. Sally sipped her sherry. Davis sipped his whiskey.

Sip, sip.

As the alcohol warmed and relaxed them both, a relationship budded. They stopped avoiding each other's eyes. Davis smiled again, totally charming.

'I told Justinian this room is very nice. Did you design the decor?' Davis said.

Sally sensed he was genuinely enthusiastic and a part of her, a part she had kept buried since his birth awoke. She liked Davis instinctively. She wasn't sure if her feelings were maternal, or simply a reaction to his natural charm. A few more moments and they would start to speak honestly and without embarrassment.

Justinian shouted in the kitchen, 'Damn! Go away, cat. Hell spawn. Your mother was a camel. Sally! Help!'

She was half-way across the room before she turned to Davis. 'I'm sorry, I'd better go to him.'

'Of course,' said Davis, half-rising to his feet. 'Can I help?'

'No.'

She left him and Davis sank back to the sofa. He thought of grabbing his coat and bolting for it. The cat, so eloquently banished from the kitchen, clawed his leg and jumped onto his lap. After a moment's hesitation, Davis stroked him. He wondered about his mother. He had the impression that the curiosity and warmth waking in Sally was being stifled by her wish to return to normality.

At dinner Davis decided he had to succeed here. Perhaps it was the recent loss of his mum, but it was important that Sally at least want to see him again after tonight. He knew he would be fond of her. He wasn't sure about her husband. He was strange, but after the first bottle of wine, he got the measure of Justinian's humour

They exchanged biographies. Davis was an advertising executive, well-heeled and with a bright future; a son to be proud of.

Sally was a magistrate and a doer of good works locally.

Justinian tended the garden, bees and the cat. He was regarded as eccentric in the village.

Justinian asked Davis' marital status. Davis enthusiastically brought out his mobile phone and showed photos of his fiancé. Justinian hid his disappointment.

They entered the lounge to be greeted by the disgruntled cat. He had been firmly excluded from the meal and the fire allowed to die. Justinian set about lighting it with the meagre supply of logs.

The others watched until he'd finished, then he turned and looked at Davis.

'My dear boy, I think, you can remove the tie now. May I see it?'

Davis undid the tie and handed it to him.

'Very nice silk.'

Rather than hand it to Davis, Justinian folded and placed it on the coffee table in front of him. As Davis had a brandy in one hand, he let it lie.

'How did you find me?' said Sally. She meant: "Why?"

'My mother, er, Mrs. Land, died two months ago. She left a letter.'

'She promised she wouldn't,' said Sally.

'I know', said Davis. 'She said so in her letter. She said that I had the right to know. Then of course, what with Facebook, she said she thought I might accidentally come across you. She'd seen a lot of stories about people finding each other, in the papers. It worried her.'

Sally thought for a moment. 'I hope you don't take much notice of newspapers, Davis.'

Davis sat forward, hunched, with his elbows on his knees. 'Well, you know.'

'I think,' said Justinian, 'Davis is more interested in why a charming young woman like yourself, would give away a rather charming son.'

Justinian's glance at Davis would have made a bishop blush. Davis missed it as the cat was examining the edible possibilities of his ankle. Sally saw the look and felt nauseous.

Without looking up from the cat, Davis said: 'Actually, yes, I would like to know. It came as a hell of a shock to a fellow to find ...' He paused.

'He'd been rejected by his real mother as a mewling babe,' supplied Justinian. 'Obviously, she wasn't married, then. Not the "done" thing, having bastards, then. Had to give you up. Great wrench and all. Thought she'd never see you again. She won't answer your next question.'

'"Who's my father?", you mean.'

'Yes.'

'I'd like to know.'

'No!' Sally stood suddenly. 'I won't lie to you, Mr. Land.'

The "Mr Land" cut Davis like a frozen dagger.

Sally continued, 'I really wish you hadn't come here, but your phone call, you see, came as such a surprise, I ...' She bit her knuckles.

'Perhaps, it would be best if you left,' said Justinian. 'You see,' he said pulling back the curtains, 'The snow, it snows. Not sure how long the roads will be passable. We do have a guest room, but I'd prefer it if you didn't tempt me to wander in the night.'

Sally moaned softly in disgust. Davis, at first

embarrassed, then angry, rose to his feet, fists rhythmically clenching and unclenching.

'Yes?', quizzed Justinian, eyebrow arched.

Davis, suddenly ridiculous, sat again and looked for comfort, reassurance, support, to his mother. She was choking back tears. He rose and sat beside her, but was unable to touch.

'Sally.' He swallowed. 'Mother.'

Her eyes, red with tears and horror struck searched his out. 'Don't call me that. I ... I ... please leave now, before he says something.'

'I'm sorry, I'll go.'

'And you'll never know; a life of wondering,' purred Justinian.

Davis, stayed seated. 'Look, Mr Kingsmead—'

'I am not now, nor have I ever been, Mr. Kingsmead. Graham Kingsmead died – suddenly – three years ago. We bought this place the same year.'

Davis sensed a pulsating darkness behind Justinian's words. As a child he'd stood at the edge of a cliff and looked down. Something inside him impelled him to step forward into space. A man he'd called "Dad" held him secure. Now, there was no-one to hold him. He looked at Sally and realised she'd withdrawn behind her eyes.

'You really shouldn't have come here,' said Justinian. 'I wasn't in when you phoned; I would have ... We are neither of us particularly proud of our lives. You will have gathered that I have a fondness for young men. You'll forgive me for the pass at you, but old habits die hard and Sally doesn't normally allow visitors. She accepts the way I am now. She has never accepted your birth. I could tell you of a romance, of a young couple, first love and parental and class intolerance. Except you've by now realised: I'm your father. It was a holiday romance; hot sand, hot sex. From your eyes, I can see you know what I mean.'

'I guess so. Were you in love?'

'We still are, in our modest way.'

'Why couldn't you marry?' said Davis.

Justinian paused and stood. As he did so, he picked the tie from the table and wandered, passing it through his hands. He walked behind Davis on the sofa and crouched so he could whisper from behind him into his ear.

'My son's father is my father's son. My son's father has a sister and she a brother, but aunt and uncle has he none. Sally is my sister.'

Davis felt himself step off the cliff and start to fall. As he tried to process this, he didn't really notice the tie Justinian had passed over his head until he was choking. There was blood pounding in his ears, but he thought he could hear Sally muttering, 'Justinian, please … don't.'

Davis stopped kicking and Sally repeated the phrase, 'Justinian, please stop,' over and over, as she looked at the floor.

Justinian stood and placed his hands on her shoulders, then leant down so he could comfort her, by whispering into her ear. 'Shh, Sally, shh. It's alright. Everything's back to normal. You go and do the washing up. I'll tidy up in here.'

Later, Justinian sat watching the snow fall.

Death is but the Doorway

Harry was dead. Really, truly, gone—as in: found with his brains and blood spread across the floor. I knew it, the police knew it, the whole fucking world knew it. Days later, I still didn't quite believe it was true.

A month ago, I was a very happy Honours graduate, with a degree in Egyptology and my dream job. The Trust for England had acquired the stately home Roxborough Court, which contained the largest private collection of ancient Egyptian artefacts in the UK. Harry and me, we'd been hired to catalogue them.

Harry was tall, muscular, with curly blond hair, blue eyes and he spoke beautifully. He'd been educated at Eton and Cambridge—basically, he was posh. When we met he wore jeans with a rugby shirt and I wore black combat trousers, black lace gloves, black t-shirt – with a picture of Lon Chaney's Wolfman – and had a Mohican made up of three inch spikes. There were silver rings in my ears and one nostril. At first, he dismissed me as a freak, until I proved I knew more about Early Dynastic Period hieroglyphs than he did.

I made him laugh. Later, he said he was amazed by me and shocked he'd fallen in love. One up to Cupid's arrow, I guess. Or Puck's love potion.

A week after we'd started work, we decided to explore the rest of the house. Harry wanted to know if the cellar contained any valuable wines. I liked the idea of dark, dank vaults. I pictured us exploring using candle light. Boringly, there was electricity. The cellar had nine chambers off a central corridor, each lit by a single bulb hanging from a tattered flex. The ceilings were around twelve feet high.

I was wondering if I could get permission for a party at Halloween, when I realised Harry had left the chamber. I heard him make a strangled choking noise from another, down the corridor.

'Harry, you OK?' I said.

Silence.

'Harry, if you're mucking around, there'll be consequences.'

Walking back into the corridor, I looked into the first room to my left. It was empty, though the bulb was swaying slightly on its flex. The effect of the moving shadows was deliciously creepy. By the time I'd examined the fifth room, all with swaying bulbs, and not found him, I was annoyed. In the house above, a door slammed closed. I couldn't work out how he got past me and I turned to walk back to the stairs.

'Boo!' shouted Harry, stepping from a room behind me. I span round and ran at him, one fist raised. He backed away, hands up in self-defence.

'I thought you'd appreciate the scare, Little Miss Goth Chick,' he said, grinning.

I flung myself and pushed him down the corridor. As he stepped backwards, he tripped and we both fell.

'Ow!', he said.

'I'll kiss it better.'

'Wait,' said Harry, turning his face to look at the wall. 'There's a draft here. I can feel it on my cheek. Can you feel it?'

'Draft? You're under a gorgeous woman and you're worried about drafts? This place is ancient, of course there are drafts.'

'No, wait a moment, there's something odd here.'

He gently pushed me aside and stood to look at the wall beside us. In this part of the corridor, there were chambers on one side only. On the other, wooden shelves had been attached to the wall. Looking around, we worked out there were three hidden chambers, which had been bricked up. It wasn't hard; there were six on one side of the corridor and three on the other. Harry crouched down and used the palm of his hand to see if he could find the draft again. I told him he looked like a constipated duck.

'Can you go back to the top of the stairs and see if you can create a draft, by swinging the door back and forwards?' he said.

'As long as you understand I'm Velma and not Daphne, Fred,' I said and tramped back to the top of the stairs, whistling the theme to Scooby Doo.

After three minutes of swinging on the door, my arms were getting tired and I started whinging. 'Bored now!' I said.

'Jude, get down here. You're not going to believe this. Bring a torch.'

I found a torch hanging on the wall at the top of the stairs to the cellars. When I joined him, he was clearing a section of the shelves, about four feet wide.

'Oh, you're kidding me,' I said. 'You really think you've found a secret doorway? I bet you read Enid Blyton's, *Famous Five*, didn't you?'

'I think I can see a line in the wall.' He took a folding knife from his pocket and used it to scrape away the dust from the outline of a door. Then he tapped on the wall until he found a small panel which opened to show a handle.

'Well,' he said twisting and tugging the handle. 'These

places often have priest holes or perhaps one of the old owners was a bluebeard and we'll find all his dead brides.'

'That'll be fun,' I said.

The door opened and then stuck, leaving a gap of about eight inches, impossible for Harry to squeeze through.

He looked at me, smiling wryly. 'Now's your chance to make history,' he said.

I checked the torch worked, which it did — dimly.

'If this thing goes out when I'm in there, I expect you to rip this door down and rescue me. OK?'

'Of course. Oh yeah, it might be a torture chamber or family vault, full of coffins. Perhaps it's vampires.'

'Really?'

'Just saying.'

I squeezed through the door. There was a narrow passage on the other side, about fifteen feet long. It ended in a larger room.

'Can you see anything?' Harry called.

'I was going to say, "Wonderful things", but that would be a cliché. It's a tomb, the tomb of an Egyptian Pharaoh.'

There was a loud crack, as I trod on something.

'What? What's happened?'

'I've just stepped on a dead body. A very dry, brittle dead body.'

That's when the torch went out.

I was massively impressed I didn't scream *very* loudly. I only screamed *moderately* loudly.

Harry reported our find to both the police and the head office of The Trust for England. The police left after forensics established the corpse was a couple of hundred years old.

The Trust appointed Professor Richard Kaverin to take charge of the tomb. He brought with him a half dozen students and the bitterness of an eminent historian who'd never had a series on TV. He took one look at me, at my clothes and hair, and told me to stick to the artefacts in the house. He offered Harry a position on his team. Harry refused, explaining how good I was. Kaverin wasn't prepared to listen. I was noble and told Harry he should take this opportunity. He said Kaverin was obviously an idiot and what could he learn from an idiot?

A few days later, Kaverin held a press conference in the entrance hall to Roxborough Court. He insisted his team, plus me and Harry should attend, basically so we could watch his triumph. Grinning broadly, he announced this was the most significant find since Tutankhamun. He explained this tomb contained more artefacts from the Early Dynastic Period than any other. For the first time, he'd be able to show, in amazing detail, how people lived over five thousand years ago. I swear, if he'd been a cartoon, you could've read "TV series" on his eyeballs.

'Whose tomb is it?' asked a reporter.

'That is a mystery which I'm working to solve,' said Kaverin. 'You see, there is a plain stone sarcophagus in the tomb which was empty. Further, any hieroglyphs within the *serekh*, an oblong shape, which normally show the pharaoh's name in this period, have been erased on the sarcophagus and funerary offerings. This usually means the pharaoh was disgraced.'

'So, the body found in the tomb, wasn't the mummy?' said another reporter, who had a cameraman with her.

'That's right; we believe it belongs to the 14th Earl, Lord Edward Burlinson who disappeared in 1834. He was responsible—'

'You didn't actually find the tomb, is that right Professor?' said the lady with the cameraman.

'What? Yes, that's right. As I was saying, Lord Burlinson—'

'We found it,' I said, raising my hand. 'Me and Harry.'

Kaverin looked at me with loathing as the cameras and reporters swung towards us. I smiled sweetly.

'Lord Burlinson had his head bashed in and I'm guessing it wasn't a mummy that did it. So there's a two hundred year old missing mummy murder mystery here,' I said.

Me and Harry spent ten minutes answering questions about how we'd found the tomb etc.—speaking in sound bites. When the press conference was over, the Trust for England's PR bloke chatted with me and Harry. He gave us his card and asked if we'd be interested in being joint spokespeople, with Kaverin, for the Trust. The Trust were concerned about low child visitor numbers and he thought we'd be able to communicate with them better than Kaverin. (No excreta, Holmes.) He muttered something about us appearing on Blue Peter.

The next morning, one of the newspapers used the headline "Missing Mummy Murder". I showed it to Nan over breakfast, grinning.

'It doesn't do, to gloat,' she said. 'No good will come of it.'

'Oh please Nan, Kaverin asked for it. He was really mean to me.' I think I pouted.

'You sound like a six year old, dear. And when are you going to do something about your hair?'

'The TV people like my hair. They say it's my USP, my Unique Selling Point.'

'I'd have thought the spikes would get caught in cobwebs, in that tomb.'

I opened my mouth to answer, then thought better of it.

'No Harry this morning?' said Nan.

'No, he said he wanted to do some more research on Lord Edward in the library at Roxborough Court, and he'd probably stay at his lodgings when he'd finished.'

'Well, I think it's very romantic about you and Harry. Just like that film with Boris Karloff.'

'What Nan?'

'Black and white movie; The Mummy. It was scary. Karloff played this three thousand year old priest, buried alive for trying to bring back the princess he loved from the dead. He wanted to kill her re-incarnation so they could be together. It was really quite romantic.'

I wondered just what romantic stories she'd been downloading onto her e-reader.

'They got that wrong, you know,' I said. 'The ancient Egyptians didn't believe in reincarnation. They had a really complex system of beliefs which involved your mummified body, your *ka*, your *ba*, *Osiris*, the *Duat*—'

'Really dear? That's nice. You off now, Judith? It's nearly time for the bus.'

'Nan, please call me Jude, not Judith. Even Mum and Dad call me Jude.'

'So they might dear, but I changed your nappies and rubbed ointment on your botty. I called you Judith then and—.'

'Nan, please, call me Jude. Names are important.'

'Really? We'll see if I can remember.'

'You're coming with Harry and me to dinner tonight, aren't you, Nan?'

'Yes … dear.'

During the ten minute walk from the bus stop, up the driveway to Roxborough Court, I enjoyed the morning sunshine. The forecast was for sun all day and the rest of the week. I looked forward to spending my lunches with Harry, outside on the lawn.

We had some filming scheduled for the afternoon and I used the walk to sort out things I might say, in my head. I was so engrossed, I didn't notice the police car with blue flashing lights until it passed me. For a moment I stood watching. Then I ran after it, towards the house. I wasn't worried, just curious, and wondered if whatever had happened could be worked into the filming later.

I stopped running. That was horrible. That was a horrible thought and I was ashamed of myself. Someone must be in trouble and all I could do was wonder if it would help my TV career. I felt ashamed and wanted to speak to Harry. Nan was right, I didn't like the person I was becoming and I wanted him to promise we wouldn't change.

I stood a hundred yards from the front door to the house, calling Harry on my mobile. It was still ringing as I watched Professor Kaverin come down the front steps, escorted by two police constables. He looked up and saw me. A man dressed in a suit was with them, he looked at me too. He said something to the officers and then walked towards me. As he got near, Harry's voicemail kicked in. I looked at the man's face and dropped the phone.

He told me they'd found Harry in the tomb. His head was bashed in.

I shaved my head for Harry's funeral and wore a long black scarf wrapped round it.

The priest talked about how difficult it was to accept the death of someone as young as Harry. (Too fucking right.) He said we could take comfort in our belief that God had a plan, and this was part of it. He went on to explain the pain we were feeling was our proof that we loved Harry. The more pain we felt the more we loved Harry.

As I listened, I pictured myself throwing a hand-grenade into the pulpit, just to shut the priest the fuck up. Then I wondered if I could come back later, dig Harry up, build a pyramid, or perhaps use the tomb at Roxborough Court. Yes! Put Harry in the sarcophagus, read the Egyptian Book of the Dead over him, he'd come back. That must be what happened originally, that's why there wasn't a mummy. I could raise Harry from the dead and talk to him. Anything to say goodbye and to tell him he was an idiot for leaving me. All I had to do was believe hard enough. Then I remembered the story 'The Monkey's Paw' and concluded bringing people back from the dead was a bad idea.

At Harry's parents', after the funeral, Nan and me were made welcome by his family. His younger sister was really nice. She showed me and Nan her phone and the emails about the 'Little Goth Chick' Harry'd sent her and how he'd fallen in love.

Their kindness broke me utterly. I held Nan's arm for support and she corrected people who called me Judith; telling them I was Jude.

A week after the funeral, the police left Roxborough Hall. They had no suspects and no leads. They said Harry's blood was found on one of the statues in the tomb. The injuries showed someone held his head and smashed it against the statue. Who that was or why Harry had been in the tomb overnight wasn't known.

Their initial suspect, Kaverin, returned to lead the archaeological examination of the tomb. (OK, so he wasn't a suspect, he was helping with enquiries. He was still a bastard.) He'd been released the same day as he was questioned as Letitia, his assistant, provided an alibi. He kept the job, but lost his wife. Ha ha.

Nan wanted me to take more time off work, but I phoned head office and said I wanted to go back to work ASAP. I'd told the police Harry was looking for more on Lord Edward in the library. I didn't know how much they'd looked there for clues.

When I arrived, one of Kaverin's team was already there. Joseph, a weasel faced little snipe, aged nineteen and only at university so he could get a degree, any degree. Harry thought Joseph was funny and they'd played a couple of games of frisbee on the lawns. Basically, Harry was much nicer with people than me. I missed that. We balanced each other.

'Yo, Jude, dude!' Joseph said as I entered the library. He was eating a burger for breakfast and a gob of mayonnaise was about to land on the book he had on the desk in front of him. I wanted to rush forward to save the book, but decided that would be too intimate. Avoiding intimacy with Joseph was now one of my primary goals for the day. I dreaded him deciding to give me a sympathetic hug.

'Hello, Joseph. What are you up to?'

'Well, you know, I'm here looking for clues. I don't know, something about records of the expedition of that fourteenth earl guy.'

He moved his burger so the mayonnaise fell onto the floor.

OK, one: the professor had the same idea as me. But, two: he'd sent his most useless student. So, three: he didn't think it was that important. I guessed he was still more interested in the stuff in the tomb, thinking that would make a better TV series.

I was about to ask Joseph how far he'd got when I looked more closely at the book he was reading. It was the original, limited edition of the Kama Sutra. I prayed he'd keep his hands above the desk.

During our time working at the house, Harry and me had used the library a couple of times to work out when objects had been added to the collection. Luckily, there was an index card system for the books.

No luck: neat lines struck out any titles relating to Lord Edward's expedition. The word 'destroyed' had been added to the cards. The writing was in dip pen, rather than ball point. So, not only had the hieroglyphs showing the pharaoh's name been erased, but the finder's papers were also destroyed. Kaverin hadn't mentioned in the original press conference; that the erasing of the name wasn't done in ancient Egypt. It had been done when the sarcophagus was in the house.

Someone was thorough. Someone who hadn't simply ripped up the cards, but had left things orderly. I wondered if anyone else from Roxborough Court had been on the trip with Lord Edward. I looked for the household accounts for 1834. These showed that a Robert Lyerson was Burlinson's private secretary at the time of the expedition.

I returned to the index and looked up Lyerson. I separated the card from the others and had to blink away tears. A sticky note was attached, with one word written on it: "Harry".

The reference on the card led me to a packet of papers under Lyerson's name. There was a small leather bound notebook amongst them.

I went to a desk by an open window, as far from Joseph as I could. Not that he noticed me; he was texting and grinning to himself.

It was Lyerson's journal of the trip to Egypt. Harry had left book marks, torn from his own notebook, marking four entries in the journal.

* * *

April 24 1824—Egypt

Today there has been both great news and a great frustration for Lord Edward. We have been here near three months, in this desert valley, with no sign our endeavours would yield us success, but very early this morning we came across the entrance to a royal tomb.

Lord Edward's search for a mummy, to display and unwrap for his friends in London, would it seemed, be finally accomplished. He entered the tomb in great hopes of this, as he had to move large amounts of treasure that impeded his path from the entrance to the sarcophagus. He told me he was indeed astounded, as there was no sign that grave robbers had found this place.

Great then, was his anger when we opened the stone sarcophagus to find it empty.

He drank to excess this evening and emerged from his tent around nine, to tell me he had decided to take all that is movable in the tomb back to his home at Roxborough Court, where he will recreate the tomb, as an attraction for his guests.

Concerning the wall paintings, I am to hire an artist to make copies of these, which the same artist is to then recreate in England. All this is to be done in the utmost secrecy, as his lordship seeks to ensure his announcement of the opening of the tomb will shock and amaze his friends and London society.

His Lordship has said he will also hire an Egyptian scholar in England to translate the hieroglyphs in the tomb, as none here are able to do so.

May 23rd 1824—Egypt

Our preparations are almost complete. We have sent the majority of the items to England already, by various routes, so as to not arouse suspicion. His Lordship left last week, so that he could accompany the sarcophagus back to Roxborough Court.

I am to accompany the last large items, which are two statues of one of their gods. These were found at the entrance to the main burial chamber, we assume placed there as guardians. They are a little over eight feet tall and have a disturbing effect on me when I regard them. They are made from a stone called, so my Lord informed me, diorite. This blackish stone has been polished and gold leaf added to certain parts, such as the kilt, head dress, the mace and spear which they hold. The head is some form of animal, which has square horns and a curved snout. There is gold for the whites of the eyes, which appear most malevolent. There has been some damage to these heads, which causes them to appear as if the flesh has decayed.

August 13th 1824—Roxborough Court

It is a sad day, as we have heard most terrible news of our friends from Egypt, who came here to recreate the tomb. In order to keep the secret of his find as secure as possible, his Lordship hired Egyptians to come here to do the necessary building works. This included the young painter who recreated the wall paintings. There was some resentment from local tradesmen who wondered that his Lordship should deprive them of labour, but I believe his Lordship's stratagem to have been sound, as only the painter spoke any English and he was instructed to only converse with myself or his Lordship.

Today we learned that the ship carrying these fine men home to Egypt, has been lost in a sudden storm in the English Channel. All hands perished.

August 14

I believe I shall die soon. His Lordship has been murdered and I think the monster which did this will seek me out too.

I have removed all mention of the name of the tomb's owner that I can find, for his name must never be spoken. I did this on the instruction of the eminent Egyptologist, Sir Arthur Farnsworth, who was here this morning. He has told me he is returning to London, to set his affairs in order.

Before he left, he helped me seal the vault and hide its existence. To our shame we left the body of his Lordship in the vault and I am to tell the staff they are dismissed and that he has left for France. I do not expect to live long enough to have to answer more questions.

It is noon and grows very dark.

I shuddered as I read the last entry. Then I realised a cloud must have blocked the sun, as it was darker outside and a cold draft came from the open window.

As I was leaving the library to find Kaverin, Joseph asked if I was going to the gala reception the next evening. It was being held to welcome 'The Director of Antiquities at Cairo Museum'. A long title for a short man, judging by the documentaries I'd seen him host on TV. I told Jospeh I was and bolted before he had a chance to ask me for a date.

Kaverin was in the tomb and looked irritated when he saw me. I explained about the journal. He listened and then silently took it and read the marked pages.

I stood with my hands behind my back, feeling as if I was being interviewed by a head master. I looked at the floor and the statues. There was no sign of Harry's blood.

After he'd finished the marked sections, Kaverin started reading other passages. I wasn't sure if he wanted me to stay, but I had no intention of leaving him before I'd got a reaction. I relaxed a little and walked to examine the wall paintings, which I'd not seen since he'd arrived.

One section showed a man losing an eye to a black boar. The scene was graphic by Egyptian standards, as one of the tusks of the boar was in the eye socket. Another scene showed the one-eyed man dismembering another man. At the corner of this scene was a black cobra.

I recognised the story. It showed Horus, losing his eye to his uncle Set. Horus later killed Set and cut him into fourteen pieces; as Set had done to his brother Osiris— father to Horus. Set escaped Horus by leaving his body and adopting the form of a black snake.

I wondered if, assuming we ever found the mummy, it would have only one eye. That would make this place even more extraordinary. This might be the actual tomb of the historical Horus, who inspired the later myths.

Kaverin looked up from the notebook.

'Well,' he said, 'I have to congratulate you Jude. This is indeed another great find.'

'Our find,' I said. 'Harry and me.'

'Yes, of course.'

I left, to tell Nan what I'd found.

Nan listened carefully as I explained how I'd solved the mystery of the missing mummy, kind of, and why Harry might have been in the vault. He'd obviously worked out something from Lyerson's journal. We still didn't know who'd killed him.

Nan listened and then thought for a moment and said: 'So, Jude, dear. What exactly is the difference between a grave robber and an archaeologist?'

'Harry said it was just a matter of timing.'

'And what about people's beliefs?' said Nan. 'They believed in the afterlife and them needing their bodies preserved and all the things in their tomb. Seems a shame if they come back with Osiris and find themselves in the British Museum or wherever. It'll be confusing for them and I imagine a few of them will be very annoyed.'

'You've been watching the History channel, haven't you Nan?'

'Yes dear, there was a very good program on, which explained how Egyptians needed their mummified body and their name, and a ba and ka, I think. Fascinating how they thought their double, their, ka could inhabit the statues placed in the tomb. I was just wondering how long does belief last for, how long is it real? I know the grave robbers took the gold and left the mummies, well, because they thought it wasn't right to hurt them. But, you and your archaeology friends, you don't seem to care. I know no-one holds those beliefs anymore, but think Jude, they believed they were right for over three thousand years. That must have some effect, mustn't it?'

The television crackled and hissed in the front room, the volume suddenly blaring and then it went quiet.

'That damn telly, it's been doing that off and on all day today,' Nan said. 'It must be that funny weather we've been having; atmospherics. Look outside, at how dark it's got.'

'Summer storm. It's been so hot recently, it had to break sometime,' I said.

The gala started with a champagne reception in the Great Hall at Roxborough Court. Nan and I stood with the hundred other guests, juggling drinks and small quiches, beneath displays of ancient weaponry on the walls. The air was humid and oppressive.

I looked stunning in my black mourning dress. My

head was still shaved and I'd painted the eye of Horus symbol around each eye. It was important to me that I be here for Harry, looking my best.

Letitia, Kaverin's assistant came and spoke to us. I liked her; but not her taste in men, obviously.

'How's the professor doing?' said Nan.

'At the moment, he's having a row with The Director of Antiquities. Richard is insisting he should announce the name of the tomb's owner. The Director's not happy about it, he thinks there's more research to be done.'

'Is it Horus?' I said. 'Is he going to announce the tomb belongs to Horus? I've seen the paintings and wondered if that's what they meant.'

Letitia looked at me quizzically and was about to reply when Nan said, 'I know him, that man talking to the Professor. I was watching him on the telly, talking about ancient Egyptian beliefs, yesterday. I told you, didn't I, Jude?'

'Yes, Nan.'

Further conversation was stopped by Kaverin striding to the small stage and the microphone.

'Ladies and Gentlemen. My apologies for the disturbance. My esteemed colleague and I have a slight difference of opinion. However, I'm convinced that what we have in the cellars here is indeed an astounding discovery, greater than I'd originally imagined.'

He then spent five minutes explaining the background to the find, thanking sponsors and generally being quite boring, so that whispered conversations were beginning to break out further from the stage. Sensing this, he hurriedly changed tack.

'So, it is with great pleasure, I'm able to announce, despite the views of others, that we have here; the tomb of the historical pharaoh who came to be known as the Egyptian god Set.'

He spread his arms wide, lifted his face and called 'Oh
Set – life, health, strength be to you!'

'Now,' said Nan. 'I don't think he should have done
that.'

There was enthusiastic clapping and whistles from
Joseph and the rest of Kaverin's team, whilst the
dignitaries who'd been invited, were more reserved in
their applause.

Joseph started a chant, which Kaverin's team took up.
'Oh Set – life, health, strength be to you!'

Kaverin smiled, triumphant, until we heard the
scream from the cellars. Moments later, a young woman
stumbled into the hall, blood splashed across her face.

'They killed him,' she said to the first person she found
by the door; Joseph. She clung to him and he hesitantly
embraced her, trying to work out what to do with his
mobile phone.

Lightening flashed and thunder rumbled immediately,
the storm was directly overhead.

The Director and Kaverin pushed through the guests
so they could question the girl. Naturally, most of the
guests also moved towards the door. Nan pulled me back
from joining them.

'Jude, we should get out of here.'

'Why?' I said.

The room became quiet, as people heard a rhythmic
sound from the cellar. It was footsteps, very loud
footsteps; the sound of stone falling on stone.

Some people near the door to the entrance hall ran
towards the main entrance. Then people started moving
back into the hall.

Joseph and the young woman, who'd passed out, were
left by the door. He looked up at the two figures who
entered. They were the eight foot tall statues of Set from
the tomb. I'd have just run. Joseph stood, making sure he

was protecting the woman. The nearest statue swung its mace and crushed his skull. Idiot, brave beautiful idiot.

The Director stood his ground and started to speak in Egyptian. The other statue speared him. Kaverin gibbered, until a mace smashed the side of his face, forcing the eye from the socket.

One of the men grabbed a large battle axe from the wall and swung at the nearest statue. The blade connected with it's torso and shattered. The statue paused, looked at its attacker, grabbed him by the shirt front and then tore out his throat with its teeth.

The statues herded us into a corner of the hall which had no windows and no door. The floor was slippery with blood, shit and piss. There were whimpers, pleas for mercy, prayers to gods not heard of five thousand years ago and gradually, fewer screams as the statues continued the killing.

Notes from lectures, images from the tomb and Harry's face tumbled through my mind. I reasoned the Professor had originally spoken in English, which seemed to trigger this insanity.

I stepped forward from the crowd, pointing to my eye make-up, saying: 'I am a high priestess of Horus, who vanquished thee. I command thee to return to whence you came.' Using "thee", rather than "you" seemed more magical to me.

The statues paused and looked at each other. The one closest to me, curled its lip into a silent snarl and dropped its mace. The guests quietened as most held their breath.

I relaxed slightly. 'I command thee—'

The statue grasped me by the throat and lifted me from the floor, at arm's length. I gasped for air and kicked.

'I know you and I know your names!' screamed Nan.

The statues snapped their heads towards her.

'You are Set, the golden one, he of Nubt, Master of Storms, Lord of Chaos, I know your names and I demand you let us pass,' said Nan.

The statue let me fall. Nan knelt down to feel my neck for a pulse, keeping her eyes on the statues. Their chests moved as if they were breathing.

Nan couldn't find a pulse. She closed her eyes for a moment, and clenched her jaw to choke back the tears.

She waved everyone should go, at first people moved slowly, but once one guy had got past the statues, everyone ran, except Nan.

'I call on Ptah, who named all things and spoke them into being,' she said. 'I call on Ra, Osiris and Isis to take Set to the Duat, the land of the dead.'

The statues became absolutely still and Nan left the hall. The sky brightened. She found some men on the lawn and told them to find pickaxes and to destroy the statues. No-one argued with her.

A few minutes later, Letitia found Nan cradling me.

Letitia said, 'How did you know what to say?'

'Jude said it the other day: names are important and that nice Director man, that's what he was talking about on the TV yesterday. He said how the Book of the Dead listed the names of the gods, so people could pass them safely in the underworld. I was interested so I looked them up in Jude's study books.'

I don't know if I have a ka or ba, whether I need them or my body to return with Osiris. In life, our beliefs can make a heaven out of hell; or a hell out of heaven. I wonder if having studied The Book of the Dead so well, I've made my own path in the afterlife; that my belief has made my own Duat, my heaven or my own hell.

I know there is a dark tunnel ahead of me with a warm and gentle light at the end. That is all I know. I hope I'll see Harry again.

I look down and see Nan cradling my head, talking to me.

She says: 'Oh, Jude. What am I going to tell your mother?'

Nursery Rhymes

The blade on the pendulum is falling closer to me with each arc. I don't know how much time I have before it slices into my face or groin.

"Eeenie, meenie, minie, mo,
Cock or face are first to go?"

There are rats here. I can feel them clawing at my hands, running over my legs. I'm tied naked and there are rats.

It's very Edgar Allen Poe, isn't it? I wonder how Sinclair managed to build all this. As revenges go, it's pretty extreme. But then, I did kill him.

To be fair, he did come back.

It was Mother who opened the door to Sinclair. The first I heard of his arrival was her screaming: 'Sinclair! Oh my God, it's Sinclair!'

I had no idea what she was talking about and thought perhaps she'd finally lost it. I came downstairs to find my brother standing in the hallway, whilst Mother hugged him and sobbed into his shoulder.

'Oh darling, but you're cold, we must get you something to eat and warmed up,' she said.

'Later, Mum,' he said. 'I'm really not that hungry. I'm just glad to be home.'

'Where have you been son?' said Father. 'It's nearly a year. We were on the point of declaring you legally dead.'

'There's just a lot of darkness, rushing river water and then the next thing I remember is being in hospital. I'd been washed out to sea. No identification and no memory of who I was. It's only just come back to me. I'll tell you the details later, Dad.'

'It's a miracle!' said Mother. 'All those prayers, the countless times I asked God to give me back my son and now here he is. James, you said we had to move on, that we had to declare him dead, but look! Here he is! It's so wonderful! James, isn't it wonderful?'

'"Oh frabjous day! Callooh! Callay! I chortle in my joy"', I said.

'James, stop being so clever. You and your rhymes, you read too many books; you know that don't you?' said Mother.

She released her hold on Sinclair and he took a step towards me. I couldn't help it, I took a step back.

'It's alright, James, I used to like your funny poems,' he said, as he walked towards me. When he grasped my hand, it was so cold, so very cold. It was as if he'd just stepped out of a freezer. He pulled me close, hugging me. It was then I smelled him. We'd had rats a few months before and a couple had died under the floorboards. That's what he smelled like—a dead rat. I wondered why Mother and Father hadn't noticed, but I don't think my mother would have cared. I opened a window by the front door. I needed some fresh air to help clear my head.

'I remember you tried to save me. Isn't that right?'

'Yes, of course,' I lied. I hadn't tried to save him, I'd killed him. I know I'd killed him after I'd ... never mind. I killed him.

It was all very confusing. He was cold, he stank of death, he looked pale but not dead. He didn't shamble or make any attempt to eat our brains. That was when I realised I'd gone into shock. Thinking he was a zombie was just the shock of seeing him again.

'James,' said Father, 'Close the window, it's cold and raining outside. Sinclair, you're a bit whiffy son.'

'Yes, sorry Dad,' said Sinclair, 'I had to sleep rough last night.'

There's a clock here. As well as the sound of the machinery behind the pendulum, I think I can hear it ticking. It's large, ebony and there is blood dripping from its face. Not sure if it's the red blood dripping or the clockwork ticking, I hear. It chimes the hours in the wrong order and the hands do not move.

I've heard people who are in terrible situations, soldiers on the front line, people in sinking boats; call for their mothers. Actually, I think they call for their 'Mummy'. I don't have one. I have Mother and Father. Sinclair has Mum and Dad. Same people, different parents.

Thinking of the past is helping me take my mind off the rats.

I was sent to boarding school when I was five years old and stayed there until I went to University. My parents simply wanted me out of the way as much as possible. Being a bastard, I was an embarrassment for them both.

You see, my father wasn't exactly in love with my mother when I was born and they certainly weren't married.

One night, he persuaded her that as they had nowhere else to go, his car – in a dark, muddy, country lane – was as romantic as it was going to get. I have occasionally speculated what it must have been like, in that car, with the windows steamed up. Apparently, it was a very nice

BMW with leather seats. I wish I'd never known that, as I can't help thinking about the rhythmic sound of creaking leather and the difficulty of removing stains. Perhaps he had a travel rug ready. If he did, no doubt the travel rug had served a similar purpose in other dark country lanes. After all, it was a company car and he was a good-looking young salesman.

Father and Mother saw each other regularly after that first time, as she proved both enthusiastic and adept at the spatial awareness necessary for these fuckings. For her, this was a rebellion against her privileged and very formal upbringing. For him there was the thrill of bedding the boss' daughter. They continued like this until my mother informed him she was pregnant and not about to have an abortion. He promised her faithfully that he would stand by her decision. He left within an hour.

It took my grandfather eight months to find and persuade him to come back, by which time I could have attended their white wedding.

All this I learned in a school holiday, listening to after dinner drunken recriminations. It didn't matter that I heard, as I didn't really count. I lived at the periphery of their vision.

I think my brother's birth saved their marriage. Perhaps it was those magic words, "Our son," with the added layer of respectability that wedlock provided. That and Sinclair's blue eyes, blond hair, grace and utter charm. A real chip off the old block. By the time he was a teenager, it was clear he had the same way with women as my father.

Sinclair was not sent to boarding school. We met only briefly at Christmas holidays, when I could admire the more extravagant presents he'd receive. Summer holidays I spent with my grandparents, whilst my parents and Sinclair holidayed abroad.

Guess what: I was bullied at school as the boy whose parents didn't love him. So, yes, naturally I read books; lots and lots of books. Books weren't my friends, it would be ridiculous to think that, as friendship requires dialogue; but they were my solace.

I got a first class degree in computing and my grandfather, who obviously felt sorry for me, gave me a job at the family firm. Don't get me wrong. He didn't like me or feel any particular warmth. He just felt it was the right thing to do for one's family. Still, decent enough of him to insist I move back into the family mansion.

Neither my parents or Sinclair congratulated me on my First.

There is an eye watching me. It is magnified in one of the walls. A pale blue eye. Perhaps it is Sinclair's watching to see if I'm dead yet. The ticking has moved. I can hear it from beneath the floorboards.

There are whispered arguments. I hear them talk of burying me whilst still alive or throwing me into the pit, which they say is near me.

I see his game now. He's intent on driving me insane. He won't kill me. He can't, it would be too messy, too difficult to explain how I was split in half. He will not kill me; he's just trying to scare me.

Gears shift and the blade drops a few more inches towards me.

"Here comes a candle to light you to bed,
Here comes a chopper to chop off your head."

A year ago, there was a sales conference. Sinclair was the company's Sales Director in my grandfather's firm. My father was Managing Director—the obvious sweetener that brought him back to marry my mother. In Sinclair's words I was just a data monkey, working in the Management Information Systems department. In his eyes, I'd only been at the conference as I'd been the analyst who'd prepared the charts and slides. However, Grandfather liked us all to be at these things—except Mother, of course. As much as she might have wanted to see her darling boy inspiring the sales force with twinkling eyes and charming wit – occasionally at my expense – there was no way my grandfather and father would let her curtail their fun at the evening celebrations. Everyone knew that what happened at the sales conference, stayed at the sales conference.

I found the evening boorish, but any complaint I had against Sinclair's cronies would simply be ignored. They sickened me and I left for my room as soon as I could. I ensured the door was locked and chained so I could read undisturbed.

Next day, Sinclair had to be at Heathrow airport at seven a.m. for the flight to South Africa—a year end incentive for him and the top three sales guys. It had been agreed, by which I mean: I'd been told, I would drive him the three hours from the conference hotel. The others would go by mini-bus.

It was still dark and he was still drunk as we left. There was torrential rain. The stink of alcohol from his skin nauseated me. Fifteen minutes into the journey, he asked me if this lovely, leather upholstered BMW, reminded me of anything.

'No, Sinclair,' I said.

'Are you sure, James? I mean, I know you can't possibly remember the actual night, but doesn't this sound make you think of Mum and Dad?' He squirmed in his seat, making the leather creak. Slowly at first, then gaining momentum. He added sighs and groans, as if he was dubbing a porno, until he started giggling. That brought on a fit of coughing.

'Stop the car! Stop the car!' he shouted. 'I'm going to be sick.'

I slammed on the brakes, half-hoping he'd smash his face on the dashboard. No luck. He threw the door open and staggered to the side of the road, ahead of the car, so he could use the headlights to see where he was going.

I could see him leaning forward in the headlights, hands on knees retching. The rain made the scene look like a pointillist painting. Then he just slid downwards; down what must be a bank in front of him. I guess he would have yelled, but the rain drowned out any other sounds. I got out of the car, cursing him.

At the spot where he'd been standing, I looked down. A half dozen feet or so below me was a swollen and fast tumbling river. I could hear, rather than see him, so I went back for the torch. When I found him, he'd managed to grab the lower branches of a tree on the bank. From the waist down he was in the water. I was thinking I'd have to go back to the car to get a tow rope when the ground I was standing on gave way beneath me. I let go of the torch and scrabbled to hold the earth as it slid past me. The river was freezing and the rain hit me like lead pellets.

Amazingly, the water wasn't as deep as I'd thought. It only came up to my thighs and I couldn't understand why Sinclair was so submerged.

'Sinclair!' Are you there?' I called.

'You fucking moron! Why'd you fall in? Now how am I to get out?'

'I'm sorry,' I said.

I waded closer to him.

'Listen, it's not that deep, I can——'

'What! What can you do? My fucking ankle's twisted or busted' Jeesus! I should have gone in the fucking mini-bus. Those guys would have known what to do.'

'Sinclair, I'm doing my best, OK?'

'Your best? Hah! My hands are going numb.'

That's when the current took hold of me and I fell against him, pushing his head under water. He surfaced, angry.

'Christ Almighty! What are you trying to do, you wanker! Kill me?'

I hadn't thought about it until he said it and then I pushed the thought from my mind. I was better than him. He might think that – might even do it – but I was better than him. I grabbed for and held a branch of the same tree. Lightning flashed and I could see we were only a few feet from a wooden jetty. I was hoping there'd be more lightning as there were no cars passing and no lights from homes that I could see. The thunder rumbled.

'Sinclair, can you hear me?' I used my right arm to grab him under the shoulders. I wanted him to feel safe. 'Sinclair, there's a jetty a few feet from here.' I felt him look around. 'Sinclair, I need to know if you can hear me.'

'Yes, yes! There's a jetty'

'Fine. We need to get to it. I'm going to pull you there, O.K.?'

'Get on with it then.'

It was really quite easy to get to the jetty. I got there first, made sure he was holding onto one of the pillars and then I hauled myself onto the deck. I needed to catch my breath before I pulled him up. I got down on my knees and reached down. I got him under the shoulders and hauled him up.

I lay him on the deck and he started shivering violently. I lay down behind him and wrapped my arms around him to keep him warm. He began to still a little.

'Get off me you fucking queer!' He struggled slightly, but I realised he didn't have much strength.

My cock was hard. For the first time in our lives he was utterly helpless and I was in control and that made me hard. I wanted to punish him, take some of that love and security, which he'd had all his life, from him. I reached round and started unbuckling his belt. He realised what I meant to do and he twisted to free himself.

'What are you doing!?' He sounded scared and I loved that. I shouted in his ear as I entered him, though I think the thunder drowned me out:

"He took his vorpal sword in hand …

One, two! One two! And through and through!

The vorpal blade went snicker-snack!"

It wasn't just him I was screwing. There was a gallery of school bullies who I taking revenge on. I was in him and reached round to grab his balls so I could hurt him. He was hard too. I didn't want that. I didn't want him to enjoy it! I fucked him harder and put my forearm across his throat to strangle him. I started gnawing his neck, biting him, wanting to hurt him in every way possible.

I came and then stood over him. I kicked him and kicked him again. He was a rag doll when I'd finished. I listened and felt for breath or heartbeat. Nothing. He was cold. I stamped his face a couple of times, then stripped him and pushed him over the edge of the jetty into the water. I hid his clothes in the well for the spare tyre, in the car.

I called the police ten minutes later, once I'd got my story straight in my head, telling the truth as much as I could: how he fell in the river, how I'd fallen in looking for him and then found the jetty. They believed me. There was no body to contradict my story and the rain cleaned everything, washed away my sins.

That night, I felt free of him for the first time.

Something still worried me. I wanted to know if what I'd done made me gay. I looked up male rape on the internet. Apparently, I wasn't gay, which was a relief. I also found out he was hard as that's just what happens if you fuck a guy.

I wished he wasn't dead. It would have been better if he'd lived with what happened, had felt confused and ashamed for as long as possible.

I have to stay awake. If I'm still for too long the rats gnaw me.

I can feel the air from the blade as it swings past my face.

"Chip chop, chip chop
Last man's head off."

In the year that followed Sinclair's disappearance, I frequently heard tales from my parents, of what Sinclair would have done, how Sinclair was sorely missed, Sinclair this and Sinclair that. It hardly bothered me. At least they were talking to me. Slowly, he was being laid to rest.

Dinner on the night he came home was all about him. He explained how he'd been found and hospitalised for nearly three months and how, when he'd come out, he'd moved in with one of the nurses. His memory had come back only in the last day or two, although, he said, he didn't remember everything.

I sat there, listening, waiting for him to reveal what had happened that night, my heart thumping in my chest. I reasoned, that as he didn't have the police with him, he couldn't remember. Of course, it might only be a matter of time. So, I had to work out a way of killing him. Again.

After dessert, I was looking for a moment to excuse myself, so I could go up to my room to read. I needed to read, to escape.

'We must have a toast,' said Sinclair.

'We already had one, at the beginning of the meal, to your safe return,' I said.

'But this one is to you, James. To your future and our happiness as a family.' He went to the bar and poured four shots of whiskey.

'Down in one,' said Father.

So, I drank my whiskey in one shot. A minute or two later, I remember the carpet suddenly coming up to hit me in the face.

Sinclair speaks to me.

'Hello James. Are you enjoying your sleep?'

'What have you done to me?' I shout, but I can't hear my voice.

'Sorry, James, that was a rhetorical question. You can't speak as you're in a coma. Looking on the bright side: Mum and Dad are paying for the best care. You have a private room and I'm coming in to read to you as often as I can. Rest assured, I'm going to be with you frequently; so I can interfere with your medication.'

I get it now: he's managing my dreams.

"To sleep, perchance to dream—ay, there's the rub,

For in that sleep of death, what dreams may come?"

Reading from Edgar Allan Poe; he's planting images of deaths in my mind. I wonder which author he'll choose next.

I look round for a black bird sitting on a bust of Pallas Athena: a raven, which I know will say, "Evermore."

The Worst Day

Howard Shepherd and his wife were arguing over the cooling body of their seventeen year old son, Euan.

'This is your fault,' she said. 'You know that, don't you?'

'I didn't know this would happen. I didn't want this. I didn't mean ...'

'You didn't listen, you never listen. It's not like you weren't told, you bastard!' She slapped his face.

'Mrs Shepherd, I'm going to have to ask you to calm down,' said the surgeon. 'I am so sorry, but I do need you to make a decision. Do we have permission to use his organs for transplant?'

For a moment, Howard and the surgeon both thought she would hit the surgeon too. She swayed slightly and they had to catch her by her arms, as she crumpled. They guided her into a plastic chair.

'Mr Shepherd, I really am sorry, but I do need you to make a decision. Can we help others?'

He noticed the surgeon didn't say "use his organs" now, and he felt frightened by her manipulation of him. He felt frightened as she tempted him to say "yes"; just so this would all end.

He looked from the surgeon to his wife, tears rolling down his cheeks.

'He's my son. I love him ... no, no you can't.'

Then he stumbled out of the room and away down

the corridor, towards his car. He pushed past the police constable who'd been waiting for Euan to recover, so he could answer questions. He hurried by the other lad's parents. Rather than look at them, he concentrated on the posters on the wall.

When he got to the car, he looked back to see the policeman had followed him to the doors of the hospital. When he realised Howard was heading for his car, he ran after him, calling; 'Mr Shepherd, Howard, wait!'

Howard got in the car and started the engine, desperate to get home. He had to get to the computer before they started asking questions about what was on it. They couldn't know what his son may have left behind.

The rain was pouring down; which meant it was difficult for the policeman to recognise his car once he got into the evening rush hour. He chanced a short one-way street against the traffic. Leaving the city, he headed north for the village.

The further he got, the more he relaxed and the less he glanced into the rear view mirror, looking for a flashing blue light.

He started rehearsing stories for the police. They were very similar to the ones he'd told a newspaper a while back. Firstly, this wasn't cage fighting. This was mixed martial arts. This was good for the kids, they enjoyed it. It was better that they were doing this, rather than walking around the streets with knives, killing each other. Was that what people wanted: kids with knives?

He thought of the barn, with the cage—no 'arena', no 'boxing ring': then thought of the dark stains on the floor and the cameras linked to the website. Perhaps he should burn the barn. No-one would come to the fights now. Not after this.

He looked in the rear view mirror, into the face of his

son.

'Hi, Dad,' said Euan.

Turning to look into the back seat, Howard swerved into a ditch, killing the engine. He heard the rain beat on the roof and his own terrified panting, nothing else. He sat there for a few moments, not daring to look into the back seat; waiting for a cold, clammy hand to be placed on his shoulder.

He shook himself and got out of the car and looked into the back seat. Empty. He let out a snorting laugh of relief: it was just his imagination, damn it.

He stood back to inspect the damage to the car. It wasn't going anywhere. He looked around him and recognised the hill he was on. It was another couple of miles to the farm and the barn. He could cut across country and perhaps make it before the police.

It was important that Euan be seen as the victim in this, that it was the other boy who'd murdered him. He knew the story had holes, but he could work on those as he walked.

Soon he was soaked through and shivering. The ground was muddy and treacherous, but that didn't matter. He had to do this, for Euan. He walked on, scared to go faster as he kept slipping in the mud. Now he was off the ridge of the hill, the heaviness of the rain and the late evening light meant he couldn't see more than ten feet in front of him.

'Hello, Mr Shepherd.'

He stopped walking and looked up from the mud. Jason, Euan's best friend, was standing in front of him, dressed in a hospital gown.

'You shouldn't be here. You should be back in hospital, son.'

'Oh, I am. I'm in a coma. I just said I'd come and give Euan a hand,' said Jason.

'I don't understand.'

'It's simple, Dad. Really, really simple,' said Euan, stepping out of the rain.

'But you're … you're dead. It's OK, Euan, you don't need to worry. I'll get to the house before the police. I'll destroy the barn, wipe the computer, take down the website. They won't know you set everything up.'

Both young men laughed.

'You have no idea, do you Dad?' said Euan. 'Once something's on the web, it's there for good. Besides, you're missing the point.'

Howard looked at them, his mouth moving slightly as he tried to find words, but uttering nothing.

'Dad, how do you think we got like this?' said Euan.

Euan painfully pulled off his hospital gown. Howard looked at his naked son. He looked at the swollen eyes, only one of which was open. His lips were inflated and bleeding. His nose, bloated and twisted where it was broken. There were yellow purple bruises around his chest, shoulders, abdomen and legs. Howard looked down at Euan's feet, at his broken toes where, the doctors had told him, someone had stamped on them. Euan turned to show his back, where he'd obviously been kicked.

'Well, you two were practising,' said Howard. 'Things got out of hand … You'd argued over Rosie, I know you both fancy her … I don't know. But look, we can sort that out later. If I destroy the barn, it'll be harder to prove it was you.'

Euan turned back to him and moved closer. 'Us, Dad. It was us. You and me. Though it was your idea. Remember?' Howard saw the blood speckle from his lips as he spoke.

'A couple of years ago? Do you *remember*?' said Euan. 'Once the farm was losing money, we had to find another income. You saw that film, saw us lads with not much to do except get into street fights on a Friday night. Thought you'd do the village a favour, give us a club to go to, where we could work out our frustrations. You set up the barn. It took you a couple of months to start charging admission for your mates to watch the bouts. Then you found those web sites and decided we could do better, could make real money.'

'You said you enjoyed it.'

'I was fifteen, Dad.'

Howard reached out towards his son in a comforting gesture, but Euan stepped back. Howard waited for his son to continue, but he stood there without speaking. He looked at Jason, but he stared at him, expressionless. Howard turned his collar up and pulled his jacket tighter against the rain.

'So, who did do this to you?' Howard said.

'Well Dad, these gentlemen from your other website. The one you got Jason here to set up for you. Thanks for wanting Mum and I not to know. Thanks for "protecting" us. I had no idea there were men this desperate to earn a few dollars.'

Howard squinted his eyes against the rain, which drove more heavily now, and looked beyond Euan and Jason. Shadows shuffled forward, becoming more substantial as they closed on him.

'I guess you knew they were beating their friends, neighbours, brothers? Did you choose the categories? "Fathers fighting sons"—was that your idea? I understand twins are popular. But of course that's not where the money really lies. Forget late night TV, forget sex and death in ancient Rome, you provided the real thing, didn't you Dad? Ah, well, you die and learn.'

There were perhaps twenty of the shadows. Bloodied, faces puffed, eyes gouged or missing, jaws swinging loose and all with raw knuckles. None of them looked strong. Howard reasoned these were the losers and was ashamed Euan had let himself be beaten.

He looked at these echoes of men and found he wasn't afraid now. He knew these were just ghosts or his imagination. He thought it was his own guilt, triggered by the shock of watching his son die. Either way, they meant nothing and could not harm him. He started walking again, towards the barn where he'd find petrol. So what, if Euan and Jason were right that the sites would still be on the web? It's not like he'd used his real name when setting these things up.

Howard was shocked when the first blow actually hurt. It was like the 'dead arms' he used to get at school. The thug who tormented him most knew the trick of protruding the knuckle of the middle finger, supported by the thumb. It was useless on bone, but punched into the upper arm, it was much more painful than a plain fist. The blow was so physical, he realised his attacker was real. That made him angry. He was no bloody victim. He'd been in the cage a few times himself.

He twisted his body so he could put his full weight behind the blow. His right fist shot out and he knew that when it crushed the gristle of this guy's face, it would feel good and there'd be a satisfying crunch. He exulted in this and felt so alive, in control. He would beat the world to a pulp and these losers wouldn't stand a chance. He stumbled forward as his fist passed through the rain in front of him.

He felt a blow to his belly and started to fold forward.

'No,' he whispered, concentrating on disbelief as if it might protect him. He straightened up and looked for his son.

'Euan, please, this isn't fair. How do I fight these—'

His arms were grabbed and stretched, so he stood

cruciform. Euan slapped him across the face twice and then stood back whilst the others delivered the beating. Somehow, he could tell the blows which were delivered by professionals and those by amateurs. When his legs gave out, he was kneed in the face, his head snapping back.

He spat blood and tried to focus on how he could escape this.

'Stop,' said Euan.

He was pulled to his feet and groggily lifted his face to look at his son.

'Euan, thank you.'

'For what? You're not going anywhere. You've just been tenderised.'

Euan punched his sternum. Howard didn't understand. The blows weren't as powerful as the others and not as painful. You boxed for the soft belly, so this made no sense.

Euan was hitting him slowly, methodically. He built a rhythm: one-two, one-two. At first, he watched his father's eyes, looking for the reaction, smiling when his father groaned.

Then he looked down to concentrate on the blows. One-two-one-two. The speed of the blows increased.

Howard felt sick and at first couldn't understand why his left arm hurt so much. The pain roared and he just wanted it cut off. As he was concentrating on this, he didn't notice when Euan ceased hitting him and his heart stuttered and stopped.

There was a tearing as his body fell forward. Still held upright, he saw the back of his own head fall away from him, then his shoulders and back drop forward, until he was looking down at himself, his face in the mud.

The pain stopped.

There was a light just beyond Euan. Howard could

feel the warmth, comfort, salvation and joy in it.

He stepped forward and was pulled back.

Euan slapped him across the face and it stung. He was punched in a kidney and it hurt. He saw the light fading as his beating continued.

The Beast In Beauty

Mikey likes the hunt. Armoured in his designer clothes, his designer body and hunger for the ache of danger. Touch the membrane titled danger, feel it give, as you dare yourself. A warning flashes and you tease the excitement, play with it, let it build, 'til it carries you through the meniscus. Drink the draught of horniness and reach to sleep with the gods. Mikey likes the hunt.

Since the poisoned blood he is, of course, more careful. Protection, extra strength, faintly outlined in his pocket.

He pads the shadows, his red Reeboks and shimmering tight cycling shorts, tanned skin, bright eyes, eager looks an invitation: to the soft, salt sweat smelling, muslin tender Shadows on the blasted Heath.

Both Hunter and Prey. Pray for that touch and reassurance, pray they're safe and pray you don't leave alone. Match your looks against the measure of the shadows. Youth an advantage, nineteen years your ally, a pleasing smile your weapon to stab stab stab, to the heart of their terror of rejection.

He steps into a clearing, under the full moon: a glimpse of faerie. A few more steps and he doesn't know why he pauses, looks up; looks at the moonlight bathing the trees, casting the shadows. Casting runes and dice—it's all chance. Chance you'll win, chance you'll lose and chance, I mean it's happened to friends, lots of friends, happens all the time—you'll meet, you just might meet ... your Dark Prince, your dream, your true, true love, cleaving unto you only, till death do you part, and for a butterfly—death is tomorrow.

Mikey looks at the moonlight bathed grass and smiles. No, never happen, not here. This is the place of Passion and Anonymity and that, has nothing to do with Love. Love is Friendship, the Quiet Magic, and here, you don't ask names.

The spirit he's drunk, sways him, makes him feel the only reality is touch. The only touch your body against the hot summer night air and the craving for another, not to share—just to supply.

The moon bathes the grass and trees in light.

'Has,' Mikey wonders, 'has anyone ever: "bathed in moonlight"?' The thought stumbling, stems the flood. If not, then he will be the first and if not the first then; every fruit must be tasted.

He lifts his beauty to the pock marked Moon and runs his palms across his face and through his hair as a man, spitting the water of the shower, shakes himself from last night's pleasures.

He slowly rubs his hands across the back of his neck, across his chest, his hands slicked by the jewels of sweat. He watches and the muscles of his stomach shift as he moves his hands across them. Stretches an arm towards the moon and protects himself from the beating moonbeams, blinks them from his eyes, as he turns his head and soaps with the clearest soap; the pit of his arm and sees the fine hairs on his forearms, washed in drops of moonlight, plate his skin in silver and he does not pause in running his hands over his body, and he does not pause, as he becomes aware of the music.

It is just beyond the touch of hearing, the substance of passion's breath, the sound of dust scraping across the

fibre of the reed. An aeolian fluid so subtle, it flows with
his blood and he's not sure if he's moving to the music,
or with the music, or is the music moving him? Who is
the dancer and who the dance? And he can touch the
music, and his movement becomes faster, and now he is
dancing, and the Music is approaching, and he wants to
meet it, and he leaps and lands and turns and looks at
the dark trunks of trees, and he can hear the Music
approaching, and sees a figure and he rushes to it, and he
stops.

He's suddenly shy.

And the Music continues.

He says, 'Hello'.

And the Music approaches.

His hand is taken and his dance joined.

And Mikey's invitation is accepted.

The dance is ecstatic: a pirouetting and leaping with
the sheer joy of being. Everything, every thing, is now
and the rhythm, the electricity, pulses in him.

The dance continues and later a terrified dying.

'Sirens', thought Sylvia, were mysterious entrancing
women, who lured men onto the rocks by the beauty of
their song. Whoever named the machines that emit a
banshee wail, to warn of approaching authority or help,
was either a lousy scholar or had a sense of the
ridiculous.

She tried to nourish the thought, but the vision of the
remains rose and she wanted to upchuck.

'OK, constable, you can turn that fucking thing off
now, we know you're here and late,' called a middle aged
man in a sports jacket, approaching the police car.

'Sorry Miss,' said a young detective constable, smiling
an apology. He was standing, she sitting on a fallen tree,
so she had to look up to reply.

'It's alright honey, I've heard worse.'

A difference in their accents, his polite British, hers Mississippi; brought the bile of homesickness.

She took a long drag of her cigarette and hated the taste of it. She noticed him watching her look of distaste. She smiled. 'Sure was a bad day to give up smoking.'

He chuckled. It was a pleasant sound. She looked closely at his face, trying to erase the other. She noted the freckles, dark brown eyes and assumed he could be no more than twenty-five or so. He was smartly dressed and reminded her of someone from some British TV show … 'Brideshead Revisited?' She couldn't quite remember.

'What's your name honey?'

'Benjamin, uh Ben Price, Miss Carroll'

'Are you … married?'

'Uh, no.'

He looked embarrassed, wary of the danger of an emotional attachment, formed whilst she was in shock and he might just be right. Some men carry their boyishness well, this Ben was one of them. She wanted to hold and protect him and imagined he'd love with that intense boy's passion. A passion to prove you're a man: you can give pleasure and, so … be a man. Soon spent, but flattering. She'd never wanted so much to be held. She wanted warm breath on her neck, comforting love nothings and a physical statement that she was still, really, here. The only breath on her neck was a cloying breeze and she pictured a hooded skeleton, behind her, that wanted to embrace.

She shivered and looked behind her. The pulsing blue lights on the police cars obliterated the moonlight—the blue grey ghosts of trees shown and dismissed.

'Alright?' Ben said.

She looked back at him. He'd crouched in front of her so their eyes were level.

'Yes, just imagining things.'

'It's the shock, I expect. Look, that's the Doctor arriving. I'll see what's happening, try and get you away from here. I'm afraid they'll want you down at the station for a statement. Will you be alright for a few minutes — on your own?'

'I'm not sure I'll ever be "all right" again.'

She looked down and shook her head quickly.

'Oh forgive me, I'm being a tad melodramatic. It's that good old Southern belle blood o' mine. Momma always said I shoulda gone on the stage.'

'I can stay if you prefer.'

'No, no, you go on honey. I'm gonna have to deal with this sooner or later, might as well be now.'

He walked quickly to the older man in the jacket. They both turned and looked at her as they spoke.

She didn't like the way Jacket looked at her. The movement of his eyes across her body, reminded her too much of a fried egg, as it haltingly slips from the pan onto the plate.

'Well, Sylvia Carroll,' she muttered to herself, 'your Momma always told you: "The Lord God gives you a blessing, he gives you a curse."'

Her beauty. Her accursed beauty. Women hated her, men assumed she was dumb, though she wasn't blonde. She should be grateful. She knew she should be grateful.

Jeeesus, she sure was feeling sorry for herself. Come on girl, you're letting this get to you—think positively: your modelling career paid for this trip to London, and you've your own agency, all 'cause of your beauty.

And she'd found, or been found by David. She missed him. Widowed a year since and she was still wandering around, like there was a limb missing or something.

She remembered their meeting at 'Ole Miss'; the university in Oxford, Mississippi, one lunch break in fall.

He'd just kept staring at her and smiling every time he caught her eye. Long brown hair, a dimple in his chin. Perhaps he was slightly fat in the face, but he was only in his first semester, he'd thin out. Besides, his grey eyes kinda made her tremble. She liked the way he looked in a cut off t-shirt. He stroked his belly and stroked a fire in her.

He was sitting with others, their talk of try outs and ballin' girls didn't seem to interest him. They didn't notice his inattention to their talk: he was still part of the group, still linked to the others. At first, his constant staring had made even her nervous, and she was used to boys staring. Eventually, he got up, walked towards her, sat opposite, continued to stare at her and smile.

'I'm going to be a famous photographer and I want to photograph you', he'd said.

She'd laughed out loud, clutched her books to her chest in disbelief.

'Well, Mercy! Do you use that line on all the girls? And do they believe you Mr High and Mighty, Famous Photographer? Or did you think I look so gullible, it might be worth a try?'

'None of the above,' he'd said, 'and if you'd like to come, with a chaperone of course, to my room, I can show you.'

He'd smiled again, wrote her a note with his name and number, got up and returned to his friends. They'd immediately demanded knowledge of the conversation, with associated gestures and looks in her direction. He'd not answered them, just read a book until they got bored.

She'd gone to his room, with a chaperone, three days later—determined not to appear too eager.

Today, she still didn't know if she'd loved the photographer or the man more. He'd specialised in documentary photographs in black and white.

Leathered, toughened faces looked at her from wall and ceiling. His lens had been sympathetic and honest with them. Mostly from New Orleans, mostly black, all men. Jazz players, pimps on street corners, sailors in uniform.

'Why no women?'

'You're the first I've wanted to ...' He let the words hang. The silence strangled her giggle.

'I've watched you.'

She expected him to continue, but he didn't. Her best friend had made her excuses and left them then. They'd made love and they'd married and moved to New York and made each other famous, and she'd never found another lover like him, or another friend like him or a photographer so talented and where was he? When she needed him so much that her throat ached and eyes stung? Where was he?

'It's OK Miss Carroll,' Ben said.

He placed his hands over hers, clasped on her knees. She looked beyond his shoulder and saw two ambulance men carrying an empty body bag, on a stretcher, into the undergrowth.

'The Inspector's said you can go now. I'll take you back to the station and we'll get your statement and ...'

She wasn't listening. As he led her to a car, she only saw the remains she'd reported: a young man, probably not yet twenty. Muscular, soggy red white vest, red Reeboks—had they always been red? Beautiful hair, throat slashed, biceps chewed by an animal, thighs and buttocks gnawed to the bone, pale ivory in dappled moonlight, strands of flesh, raw meat. Imagine the hunger of the beast: biceps, buttocks, thighs; all the best cuts—eaten raw.

She sat in the car.

Dawn was adding light to the scene—un-burnishing the silver to grey. The moon, full and resting on the tree tops. It was beautiful. For a moment Ben stopped talking, and the crackled radio messages paused and Sylvia was certain – almost certain – she could hear music.

Then the pandemonium.

'Tell me, Miss Carroll—what do you know about Satanism?'

'Whadda you mean honey?'

'Have you ever been involved in rituals, that might be thought pagan?'

Sylvia laughed, incredulous. 'You mean: "Are you now, or have you ever been a Satanist?" Oh please, Inspector, you cannot be serious.'

Detective Inspector Neal repeated the question.

A middle aged man from Yorkshire, he seemed unlikely to joke. He ran his hand over his forehead and then across his lank hair. His face was flushed from the heat, his collar undone, patches of sweat at his armpits were seeping into the lining of his jacket. He'd take it off, but those patches on his shirt were embarrassing.

He watched the suspect's eyes, as she denied all knowledge of witchcraft. He'd interviewed her for nearly an hour and her story, in fact everything about her, was solid. It were her beauty, gave her that assurance.

By God, she were attractive. Women like that though, made you feel inadequate, real pecker shrinkers that sort. Handcuff her and show her—that'd teach her. Make her understand, she should respect him. By God, the room were hot. And why were she always smiling at Ben Price? Young bastard, still wet behind the ears.

For a moment, he saw himself in her eyes. Something dirty about him, as if what she made him feel was wrong, unclean. He was a Man for God's sake, a Man! He still had a good physique, for a forty-two year old. When he slipped his shirt off, for a tart, they still smiled, still knew enough to be impressed, still knew they had a man in their arms.

Oh, sod it. Send her packing and get some rest. She'll break another day.

Neal unconsciously tugged the ends of his jacket sleeves and straightened his tie.

'OK, Miss Carroll you can go now,' Neal said. 'We'll need you to give evidence at the inquest. I'm afraid you'll have to stay in touch with us till then. Price will show you out.'

Five minutes later Ben Price joined Neal in his office.

'Well lad, what do you think about her? I mean apart from the obvious?'

'She was pretty cut up. I don't know. She doesn't seem the type, but I'm not sure what the *type* is. How does one know a Satanist?'

'Aye, that's the trouble. OK, let's look at this closely. We've had ten cases of desecration, in Highgate Cemetery, of recent graves, probably involving grave robbery. Last night, we found evidence of a Satanic or other pagan ritual, where we found something that looks like a giant egg shell. Oh, God I hate the weird ones. Also, we've got our third dead poof—'

Price winced at the word and Neal caught the look.

'Alright then; "our third deceased young male, who may, or may not, have been a homosexual". And now this cannibalism.'

'We don't know it was cannibalism Sir, I mean it could have been a wild animal.'

'So now you're telling me, not only have we got Satanists and a poof killer, though the two may be linked, but we've also got a mysterious animal that eats corpses! This is Hampstead Heath we're talking about lad, not bloody Dartmoor! Please Price, do me a favour and don't spread that story. I've already got threats of

Gay vigilante groups; all I need is an open season on every pet dog on the Heath.'

Neal wiped his brow with a grimy hanky. God, he were tired.

'Have the shrinks given us a psychological profile of the killer yet?' said Price.

'Oh, aye lad—plenty. Our man is either: a repressed homo himself; a necrophiliac, a cleanser of Sodom; as in Jack the Ripper … oh, no.'

'What?'

'What were the date of the first murder?' Neal said.

'August 31.'

'And the second?'

'September 8.'

'And last night were September 29. If we find another body today, then it looks as if he's back.

Price looked mystified.

'It's now 1989, lad. A hundred and one years since Whitechapel,' Neal said.

Price raised an eyebrow.

'Alright lad, don't worry, I'm not saying Jacky's ghost has returned to slay the pariahs of our society. But, I am thinking, some freak has decided to celebrate his hundred and first anniversary.'

Price half smiled. 'That thought, might incite an open season: on men in cloak, top hat and carrying a Gladstone bag.'

Neal, grunted his amusement. 'God, lad, perhaps I *am* losing it. It's this bloody heat. But, even if we don't find another one killed tonight, those dates are too coincidental. More than likely, he chose those dates, just to play with us; rather than comparing poofs to prostitutes.'

He mopped his brow again and rested his forehead in his hand, with his elbow on the desk. The room was silent as Price waited for him to speak. Neal looked up.

'Look lad. You go home and get some rest. I want door to door stepped up. There's too much silence about this case, too many people not telling all they know. Those nice houses in Hampstead, are hiding some nasty secrets and I want to know what they are.'

The heat made Sylvia drowsy. She had to get out of the hotel. For a week she'd gone to museums and shows and shopped and seen films, seen friends and suffered their sympathy and answered police questions and more questions, till her story had become a chant to repeat before sleep and now: she had to get out of this damned hotel.

She wanted to go back. Not to New York, but Hampstead Heath. She knew the murderer traditionally returned to the scene of the crime—what about the finder? Would she appear insane to her friends if she returned, or would they expect her to want to lay the ghost? And why the hell was she thinking about *them* anyway?

Because *appearance* was the touchstone of her life. In trouble, she looked to the china doll of her image, reflected in a mirror. She accepted her beauty would be enough to carry her through, because there would always be someone to pet and comfort her. This reflected reality was usually enough to silence the sand grain voice – the whisper of the time glass – the voice that spoke of beauty lost and ensuing loneliness.

She kissed her own cold lips in the mirror and left the room.

The taxi dropped her near Hampstead Heath station. She was so eager to see the murder site again, she had to stop herself from running, despite the heat.

She saw there was no hope from three hundred yards

away. Red plastic ribbons flapped between the trees and two policemen stood on guard. She blew a quiet raspberry and decided to wander.

Invited by the cool shadows on grass turned red brown by the hot summer, she walked to nearby trees. It was so good to be out of the hotel, among the living things. The trees around her were lush and she felt drowsy again. She lay at the base of a tree and tried to remember the last time she'd done this; spent time on her own, just enjoying herself, not having to get to a business meeting. Without her hearing it, the healing music seeped into her and she slept.

Eos was dreaming a recurring dream. He was huddled in a dark small chamber, without corners, surrounded by fluid and the sound of his own heartbeat. At first he thought he was drowning, then he was floating. Gradually, he could see light through the walls of his chamber. A soft red light flickered on the outside, tracing the veins in the wall. He could hear voices. Chanting, calling the name of his father. Then the fluid was gone and his skin and fur was wet and he couldn't breathe. He battered his horns against the walls. He couldn't breathe and it was warm. He saw a spot in the wall was turning brown, then black and an incandescence of red. He kicked with a hoof, the wall cracked and suddenly there was air to breathe and screams to hear. He stood in the ruined shell of his birth and looked around him.

Couples, mostly naked, with wine dribbling from their slack jaws, sat around him. The remaining fluid from his egg hissed in the embers of the fire .

All their eyes were wild with fear. They started scrabbling to escape his gaze, the men pushing the women to one side to escape. One woman took his gaze and he wanted her, but she was running and he needed fresh meat to eat, so he fell and falling in his dream - he woke.

He smelt the air. It was poisoned and made him feel unwell. The pools of water that he'd found, since his birth, were bitter. He looked up at sunlight through the branches of the tree. He could see the thickness of the air. It clouded his view of Helios, who seven times had ridden his chariot, across the Heavens, since his re-birth.

A tear swelled in his eye and trickled down his cheek. He wanted the fields of Arcadia as he felt so small and frightened here. This was a world of unfamiliar smells, tastes and sounds. He hated, hated, this place and the fine black dust that fell on his skin and made him sneeze.

Eos stood and stretched beneath the boughs of the tree. He ran a hand along each horn to cleanse the dust from it. He was worried and lonely. He knew he shouldn't have eaten of the beautiful boy meat. It was wrong, but his mouth watered, as he remembered the iron taste of the blood and flesh on his tongue. His tongue searched his teeth for the strand of flesh trapped near a canine, which he couldn't move. He wiped the remembered blood from his chin, as it had dribbled from his mouth. It had felt good to rub it onto his chest, to touch his nipples. Lick the drops from his finger tips. It felt good, because he had been able to *feel* for the first time in centuries. He'd been summoned to reality, and except he felt lonely; at least he could feel.

The peasants had not supplied the fresh kill, nor the wine, in the proper manner. So the fault was theirs. If he hadn't eaten, then he would have died that hour. And he had looked for other animals, had even used the pipes, but this was a dead land and none had answered.

Then he saw her. The woman he'd seen the night he was born. Walking through the trees, towards him, dressed in red. She looked tired. Perhaps if he played for her, she would not run away. Perhaps she might talk to him and tell him of this strange world. Perhaps, they might love, and she would hold him afterwards and he would stop being lonely. Only for a time.

His music worked like the charm it was and she lay near a tree. Eos, as quietly as he could, approached the sleeping woman. He lay beside her, moved his face close to hers, kissed her lips and whispered into her dreams.

Sylvia dreamed she was back in the hospital, at David's side, holding his hand. It would not be long now, his eyelids would flutter and he'd smile at her and this shrivelled thing, with its brown blotched skin and the tubes to help it breathe would say her name once and say he was sorry.

She'd spit in his face.

He'd murdered her, poisoned her blood, decreed she might poison her children. Planted a time bomb in her immune system, in the name of love, betrayed her trust, broken their vows and still she loved him.

Crying, she would wipe spittle from his face. Crying, she would leave the room for the last time.

David was a victim. A victim of those others, the catamites, the sodomites, the perverts who had seduced him; because he was beautiful, because he might further their career. It was them, not David, who had done this to her. It was on a trip to London, Fashion Week, he'd been drunk—a young man was charming.

Like "Naughty Jack", she had taken her revenge.

The dream changed. As she turned to leave David, a man, a beautiful man was standing there. His hair was centre parted and his trousers were dark brown. That he didn't wear a shirt seemed right. He was another victim, like David. She could tell that. He looked frightened and alone, almost a child. Next, he was holding her and kissing her neck. And they were in a forest and he was whispering to her, again and again:

'I saw you do it. I saw you kill the boy meat.'

There was no accusation in his voice. He was, she realised, thanking her. She looked into his eyes. They were like a young deer's, moist and without harm.

She felt the muscles of his back as she clasped him and he ran his hands beneath her dress. At his touch, a charge raced the surface of her skin. Her back rose as his lips touched the curve of her breast. Life, flowed through her veins, sensation welled and spilt.

She had to close her eyes to stop them leaping their sockets. It was impossible—she couldn't contain this sensation, as her ears rang and she wanted to gnaw on him, to possess and be possessed, and his teeth were on her nipple and the feeling moved her beyond the whining definition of pain and pleasure, because she knew he would not damage her, he was too gentle.

She thrashed, in the reins of the animal he had wakened inside her. She clawed the ground to anchor herself – she could feel the grass stalks tickle her palm, the grains invade her nails, so that she clawed the air – her anchor gone. She was bereft of time, loose of anything but her body, which was all spirit, and the spirit was fire that coruscated her spine, which arched as she pushed up to him, as she grew afraid she might never return from this experience, and if she did ... how to live afterwards?

He wakened this in her, but she felt safe.

For the words stopped, the words of 'pain' and 'guilt and 'revenge', lost meaning. Here: where meaning was an image of a shadow of a butterfly, thought was so thin you could marvel at your own hand, because you saw it new. The shadows shattered and all was light. The electric sea crashed the caverns and all was light and noise and then nothing and nothing ...

She could not move. There were no nerves that made a connection she understood. Her body was a thing at the wrong end of a telescope, which gradually focussed. But she could not move, as she looked at her lover.

Sated, her dream rolled from her and stood. He lifted the pipes to his lips and played.

And his seed grew in her.

Made in the USA
Charleston, SC
10 August 2013